PENGUIN CRIME FICTION

HONEYBATH'S HAVEN

Michael Innes is J. I. M. Stewart in private life. Educated at Edinburgh Academy and Oriel College, Oxford University, he has been Student of Christ Church, Oxford, since 1949 and Reader in English Literature at the University of Oxford since 1969. His publications include *Character and Motive in Shakespeare*, *Eight Modern Writers* (the final volume in the monumental *Oxford History of English Literature*), *Rudyard Kipling*, *Joseph Conrad*, *Thomas Hardy*, and a series of novels. Under the pseudonym of Michael Innes, Dr. Stewart is the author of a number of witty and erudite novels of suspense.

Also by Michael Innes

HONEYBATH'S HAVEN

MICHAEL INNES

PENGUIN BOOKS

Penguin Books Ltd, Harmondsworth,
Middlesex, England
Penguin Books, 625 Madison Avenue,
New York, New York 10022, U.S.A.
Penguin Books Australia Ltd, Ringwood,
Victoria, Australia
Penguin Books Canada Limited, 2801 John Street,
Markham, Ontario, Canada L3R 1B4
Penguin Books (N.Z.) Ltd, 182–190 Wairau Road,
Auckland 10, New Zealand

First published in Great Britain by
Victor Gollancz Ltd 1977
First published in the United States of America
as a Red Badge Novel of Suspense by Dodd, Mead & Company 1978
Published in Penguin Books 1979

LIBRARY OF CONGRESS CATALOGING IN PUBLICATION DATA
Stewart, John Innes Mackintosh, 1906–
Honeybath's haven.
Originally published in 1978 by Dodd, Mead, New York,
in series: A Red badge novel of suspense.
I. Title.
[PZ3.S85166Ho 1979]   [PR6037.T466]   823 .9′12   79–16662
ISBN 0 14 00.4885 5

Printed in the United States of America by
Offset Paperback Mfrs., Inc., Dallas, Pennsylvania
Set in Baskerville

CONTENTS

PART ONE

AN ARCHANGEL DAMAGED

I

CHARLES HONEYBATH HAD been out of touch with Edwin Lightfoot for years. There had been no sort of breach between the two painters, but for one reason and another the flow of sympathy between them had turned to a trickle and then dried up altogether. Reflecting on it, Honeybath (who was a reflective man) judged that here was one of the vulnerabilities of later middle age. Now one man and now the other is preoccupied with this or that; each believes that the other is turning rather dull, rather prone to slip into repetitive conversational routines sadly differing from the stimulating sparkle of yore; the intervals between meetings stretch themselves out, until eventually there has come a gap so long as to be awkward to explain. Acquaintanceships can wind themselves up more or less harmlessly in this way. But when it is a matter of friendship each party can be left feeling (quite correctly) that he hasn't behaved well.

They were, of course, different sorts of painter, Honeybath and Lightfoot, and the pattern of their careers had differed too. Neither could very sincerely have congratulated the other on the *curriculum vitae* he had elected or that had befallen him. Honeybath's had been the steadier course. As a young man he had painted portraits well, and as an old man he was painting them that way still. As he became better known his fees went up. He would have been named now by the knowledgeable as one of the top men at his

9

job; 'academic', perhaps—but hadn't Sir Joshua himself been that? Honeybath wasn't inspired or inspiring; he never had been either; all the more credit to him for preserving all his sensibility, all his integrity, through a long career.

Ut pictura—it used to be said—*poesis*; you can compare paintings with poems, and mark the same well-springs in artists as in writers of verse. Pursuing this thought, one might have said that if Honeybath was a kind of superior Robert Southey Lightfoot was a William Wordsworth of sorts—or that with a dash of Samuel Taylor Coleridge thrown in. Lightfoot's earlier career had come close to being a blaze of glory—although it wasn't, indeed, until that phase of his achievement was over that the fact had come to be widely recognized. By the time people were acclaiming 'early' Edwin Lightfoots Lightfoot himself had declined inexplicably into a seesaw between unremarkable accomplishment and disconcerting occasional vagary. He was still technically a good painter; but when people thought of him it was as a man who had once been something else.

This was very sad, and the sadder because those marvellous early works were almost oddly scarce; were by no means abundantly displayed for the delectation of frequenters of public galleries or exposed to the cupidity of collectors in the sale-rooms. Those who knew Lightfoot—and they were comparatively few, since he had become something of a recluse—were apt to declare that what had once been the power to project a unique vision upon canvas had declined into a fairly generous measure of personal eccentricity.

It has always been a canon of English society that the wealthier you are the more eccentric are you permitted to be. The poor are scarcely allowed to indulge in *outré* behaviour of any kind, unless it be occasionally under the influence of drink. Try anything more, and the neighbours turn first censorious and then nasty; the 'social services' descend on you, and after them the police. The comfortably established can be comfortably odd, and the rich may comport themselves as if they still lived in that paradise of aberrancy, the eighteenth century. Edwin Lightfoot wasn't affluent, but he had always commanded rather more money than came to him from his paintings. This was the reason, no doubt, for those phases of his career in which his productivity had been low. Moreover his wife, who was his junior by a good many years, was understood to have an income of her own. It had been a prudent marriage (such as artists are commonly supposed not much to favour or achieve), since the lady's brother was a picture-dealer in a substantial way, who had thereafter in effect acted as his brother-in-law's agent. All this meant that Lightfoot could mount a freakish turn if and when it took his fancy. In addition to which it must be remembered that artists are expected to be a little out-of-the-way. It wasn't so long ago that they were almost obliged to dress in awkward cloaks and enormous hats if they were to command the full confidence of their clients.

Charles Honeybath, although Lightfoot's exact contemporary, had the appearance of belonging to a later generation at least in this last regard. His attire had never been bizarre, and it had long since ceased to be casual either. When punctually each morning he left his modest little Chelsea flat (for he was a widower and childless) for his considerably more spacious studio not far off it might have been supposed from his appearance that his destination was some respectably managerial or directorial cubby-hole in the City. Not that he didn't own a certain presence. Take a second look, and you might conjecture that he was on his way to a studio, after all, where he was to be represented, sitting in an otherwise untenanted and slightly nebulous board-room, by that well-known limner of such spectacles, Charles Honeybath, R.A.

We now meet Honeybath, however, on his way to Edwin Lightfoot's home. This was at the instance of Lightfoot's brother-in-law the picture pedlar, whose name was Ambrose Prout. Honeybath had run into Prout a few days before at the Savage Club, and Prout had tackled him about Lightfoot almost at once.

'My dear Charles,' he had said, 'I do wish you would drop in on poor old Edwin and pass the time of day. He says he hasn't seen you for months.'

'Years, I'm afraid.' Honeybath came out with this honestly. 'No estrangement, you know. I suppose it's simply that I grow less and less sociable.'

' "Months" was Edwin's word. But probably he wasn't just being charitable. I'm sometimes not very sure that his sense of time is as it should be. But come, Charles! You surely wouldn't dump Edwin in a category of social duties?'

'Certainly not—and of course I'll look him up. Are you saying that things aren't quite as they should be with him?'

'There's nothing to be called sinister, that I can see—or not so far as his physical man goes. Hale but not hearty might express Edwin's condition. That spare type—only just short of desiccation—commonly lives to be a hundred.' Prout offered this on a faintly resentful note. He was himself a corpulent man.

'When you say he's not hearty is it in the sense that he's sunk in gloom?'

'Intermittently he's that. Of course I don't see him all that frequently myself. But he's also irritable and agitated. I'm afraid Melissa must find him uncommonly trying on the whole.'

Melissa was Ambrose Prout's sister and Lightfoot's wife. Honeybath had never greatly taken to Melissa, so this last reflection of Prout's didn't much disturb him. But about Lightfoot himself he was beginning to feel guilty.

'What does he get agitated about?' he asked.

'Oh, he just fusses over this and that, and can't stay put. There's probably some medical term for it, simply as a manifestation of senescence.'

'Dash it all, Ambrose, our generation isn't exactly in its dotage yet! And can't Edwin settle to his work? He still turns something in to the Academy year by year.'

'Well, yes—usually a portrait-sketch, or something of that sort. Pencil or pastel that he can fudge up in no time with that devilishly clever smudging thumb. But he gets down to no serious work at all.'

'I see.' What Honeybath thought he saw was the occasion of the irritable note to be detected in Prout's own voice. An Edwin Lightfoot adequately toiling in his studio more or less automatically augmented his brother-in-law's bank balance. 'But, Ambrose, why should Edwin sweat away if he has no mind to it?' Honeybath asked this challengingly. 'The man's well enough off, and your sister is said to have her little packet. Age asks ease—as some poet or other says.'

'A poet ought to know better than to say anything of the sort.' Prout's tone had changed. He was a merchant who, when speaking seriously, was always careful to regard creative endowments with respect. 'When any sort of artist stops off, Charles, he's finished there and then. He can't just get out his golf-clubs like a stockbroker, or find all his satisfaction in helping his wife prune the rose-trees.'

'Does Melissa go in for roses?' This question struck Honeybath as flippant even as he uttered it, and he realized that he was now feeling quite bad about what could be viewed as a desertion of his old friend. 'Of course I'll drop in,' he said. 'I'll take along a bottle of wine and insist on our finishing it together. It was a ritual Edwin and I had in the early days. It was usually a stuff from South Africa calling itself burgundy, and not half bad.' This time, Honeybath managed to laugh the comfortable laugh of a modestly prosperous man. 'It was two bottles, as often as not,' he said. 'We'd talk into the small hours. I remember our once arguing about the *Demoiselles d'Avignon* as if it had been painted the day before, although it must have existed before either of us was in his cradle.'

On this reminiscent note the conversation with Ambrose Prout had ended, and now Honeybath was fulfilling his promise. Only he had thought better of the bottle of wine. The gesture might have worked as a tacit acknowledgement of neglect. On the other hand it might have appeared a gesture clumsily contrived. He would do best simply to arrive empty-handed and manage an honest expression of contrition at an early stage of the meeting. Not that he must make too much of that. For the break in intimacy that had occurred was a regrettable fact for which he and Lightfoot would do best to acknowledge a joint responsibility. If they accepted this without any pother they would probably come together again easily enough. But if Honeybath were to make a to-do about his own culpability the effect might be of his elevating himself into a position of patronage towards Lightfoot the duties of which he had failed to discharge. And their relationship had never had anything of the sort about it.

These considerations accompanied Charles Honeybath as he sat on top of a bus on his way to Holland Park, and they suggest that, like most artists, he was sensitive in the sphere of personal relations. But he also had other thoughts in his mind : thoughts, as it happened, on artists in general. The serious practice of any art is obsessional, and that rather commonplace fellow Prout had been perfectly right in declaring that an artist simply can't stop off. If he does so, he virtually loses the sense of his own identity. He is, of course, luckier than most men in that society refrains from *ordering* him to stop off; from handing him a watch or a television set or an enormous cheque corresponding to his consequence hitherto in its fabric, and at the same time telling him to clear out. Society, on the whole, *likes* its artists to be immensely aged—perhaps because it feels itself safer from them when they have become eminent and doddering. Titian and Picasso, Voltaire and Bernard Shaw : their standing mounts with their years, and it occurs to nobody to tell them they ought to retire. The physicist loses his laboratory, the surgeon his beds, even the judge his bobbing barristers. But the artist goes on on his own : painting, scribbling, creating harmonies from catgut and a capful of wind.

Only—Honeybath told himself as his bus turned into Goldhawk Road—Degas' sight dims, Beethoven's ear dies on him, Shakespeare is probably bedevilled by a mounting nominal amnesia and doesn't even have Roget's *Thesaurus* to help him out. So what then? The artist too has to pack up, sharpen not his wits and sensibilities but his secateurs, and get out among his wife's roses.

Honeybath had no roses, and no wife either. He often tried to look ahead—and this present mission, which was to pick up the threads with another artist as old as himself and perhaps wearing not quite so well, put him in mind of the problem now. One could make prudent plans, and this he had done. He had put money by as carefully as any stockbroker, and a kind of old folk's home—one adequately corresponding to his station in life and his modest distinction —was already awaiting him. He wondered about Lightfoot. But Lightfoot's situation was different. He had a wife, and a wife younger than himself. He must be reckoning that, with luck, she'd see him through without any radical alteration in his domestic circumstances. Unless, of course, there were any strains and stresses in the Lightfoot *ménage* here in Holland Park that were likely to militate against that sort of easy decline into the shades.

Honeybath stood up, moved with caution along the swaying platform on which he was perched, and waited at the top of the stair until the bus jerked to a halt. Quite recently a friend of his, a famous pianist, had behaved incautiously with a rotary mower, and was now without an index finger. Honeybath had developed a mild phobia as a result of this. What terrified him was the thought of falling and breaking a wrist. If that happened they would patch it up marvellously, no doubt; within weeks it would be the same old wrist again for all common purposes. But in close proximity to paper or canvas how might it behave? The speculation was somehow even more alarming than the thought of an insidiously developing intention tremor.

He got off the bus, and set out vigorously in the direction of Royal Crescent, the abode of the Lightfoots. At this reunion, he warned himself, he must keep clear of gloomy themes.

I I

Melissa Lightfoot opened the door of the
flat. She stared at Honeybath and allowed herself a moment
of blank non-recognition before she spoke. Since there was
a good light on the landing, and since Honeybath was bare-
headed, this was either offensive or absurd.

'It's Charles,' Mrs Lightfoot said, apparently for her own
information. 'Charles Honeybath. Something must have
happened. Somebody has hit him on the head, and he
doesn't know where he's wandering. Or is he a fugitive
from the police?'

'Good evening, Melissa.' Honeybath remembered that this
sort of nonsensical banter had been Melissa Lightfoot's
notion of fun long ago. There was no particular animus in
it. She might have made just these remarks if he were calling
on his friends after no more than a fortnight by the sea.
Melissa was a tiresome woman. It was perhaps one reason
why Edwin had become (if Prout was to be believed) a tiresome man. 'How are you, my dear Melissa?' Honeybath
asked firmly. 'At least you look uncommonly well. And how
is Edwin? I'm ashamed not to have seen either of you for
so long.'

'He's asking about my husband. Shall I tell him the truth
at once? I don't see why not. Edwin's mad.'

'I'm very sorry to hear that.' Honeybath closed the front
door of the flat behind him—Mrs Lightfoot having shown
no disposition to perform this action herself. 'What sort of

madness, Melissa? It comes—doesn't it?—in so many different forms.'

'Delusions. He believes himself to be somebody else, and never the same person two weeks running. Or even *something* else. A few days ago he set up that system of mirrors you use when you're going to do a self-portrait and don't want your left ear to face the world as your right. As if it made any difference! But what appeared on his drawing-board wasn't a man at all. It was a motor-car. I wonder whether he's brought anything to drink.'

'If Edwin . . .?' Honeybath realized his mistake. 'I'm afraid not. I thought . . .'

'He used to bring something to drink. Fortunately there's plenty in the house. The two of them can talk twaddle to each other through the night, and let me get some decent sleep for once.' Mrs Lightfoot had led the way into her sitting-room, and she now sat down. 'Charles,' she asked, 'did you ever hear of a man called Flannel Foot?'

'Never.' Honeybath remembered that the third-person-singular treatment was administered by Melissa only in a standing position. 'Who is he?'

'He's what Edwin has become now. It started with a horrible journalist calling on us three or four weeks ago. He's writing something about Flannel Foot, and it seems that Flannel Foot was living in this flat when they caught him.'

'You mean he is a criminal?' By this time Honeybath had sat down too. There was no sign of Melissa's husband appearing. Perhaps he was away from home, which would mean that this awkward visit was going to fail of its purpose. Honeybath didn't know whether he would be disappointed or relieved. It didn't sound as if resuming relations with Edwin Lightfoot was going to be an easy matter. Prout had certainly been playing down the oddity of his mental state.

'Flannel Foot *was* a criminal. He died on the 18th of

December 1942, after doing five years' penal servitude to which he had been sentenced on the 2nd of December 1937.'

'Good heavens, Melissa! Where have you collected all this rubbish?'

'From Edwin. And he dug it out of some dreadful place where they keep all the old newspapers the world has ever seen. Dingley Dell, or some such.'

'Colindale. Do you mean that Edwin has been researching into the life of this person?'

'Yes, of course—and just because of this intrusive young man. Flannel Foot's real name was Vickers, and he was a burglar in a petty line of business. Children's piggy-banks and what could be got out of the gas meter. And he ended up, as I say, either in this flat or in another close by. It seems they can't be quite sure.'

'On the strength of piggy-banks, Melissa? It sounds most improbable.'

'He was pertinacious, it seems, and achieved about two thousand successful burglaries before slipping up. That's what has caught Edwin's fancy. So Lightfoot has become Flannel Foot. Only for part of the day, of course, since Edwin's madness is always a kind of bad joke. I believe he's at it now.'

'I can't hear him at it.'

'Of course not. That's the point. Nobody ever did hear Flannel Foot. Or see him, for that matter. But you *can* see Edwin. And here he is.'

Edwin Lightfoot had entered the room. He didn't look much changed. Or rather his physical man didn't look much changed. But he was wearing what might have been thought of as the Sunday attire of a respectable artisan of the Edwardian period, shiny and drab; a pair of shabby leather gloves; and a brown Homburg hat. Bright-eyed and apparently inwardly amused, he advanced soundlessly over the parquet floor. The soundlessness resulted from each of his feet being swathed in several yards of flannel. He might have been a gentleman of a past age, badly afflicted by gout.

'Charles, my dear fellow, how nice to see you! It's a shocking long time since we got together.' Lightfoot sat down with perfect ease—or at least with perfect ease of manner, since he appeared not quite to have mastered the equipment that had presumably been Flannel Foot's speciality in the burgling way. 'We really have very few visitors nowadays, and Melissa and I have to entertain ourselves as we can. She has probably told you how we've invented this little game like charades. I'm being a burglar at the moment, and she's not quite sure whether I'm after her placket or her purse. Would you care to join in? You can be Chief Inspector Thomas Thompson. "Youthful, black-haired Chief Inspector Thomas Thompson", according to the *Daily Express* of the 4th December 1937. He's my grand adversary, you know. We're like Moriarty and Sherlock Holmes. The worthy Thompson has hundreds of coppers prowling the suburbs of London on the hunt for me, but he hasn't caught me yet. It's the flannel, you see. So light a foot will ne'er wear out the everlasting flint, as Shakespeare's Friar Lawrence expresses it.'

'I'm very glad to see you keeping up your spirits, Edwin.' Honeybath managed to say this with difficulty. Although unexpected circumstances were apt to prove him a man of considerable resource, he didn't yet quite see how to tackle this situation. He wondered whether Lightfoot—this time like Shakespeare's Hamlet—was but mad north-north-west, and knew a hawk from a handsaw when other winds were blowing. But if this Flannel Foot business was a joke it seemed necessary to believe with Melissa that it was a bad one. Honeybath felt sorry for Melissa. That she was herself a tiresome woman didn't obscure the fact that her husband's freakishness—even if it was no more than that—couldn't be a thing at all nice to live with. And Lightfoot's deft rubbish about charades was alarming rather than composing. It somehow suggested the rapid cunning which the truly insane are reputed sometimes to command.

'But enough of this nonsense,' Lightfoot said. He spoke with a lightness of air that decidedly didn't ring true. 'Just let me remove these cerements, my dear Charles, and we'll have a marvellous talk.' He bent down and began unwrapping the ludicrous flannel from his feet. 'And our compotations shall be in Château Leoville-Poyferre. Business is a little slack, you know, but I can still, praise God, run to a decent claret.'

Melissa Lightfoot (*née* Prout) having already referred to the vinous resources of the household, Honeybath was prompted to wonder whether the couple had both taken to drink. He looked cautiously about him. The Lightfoots' sitting-room had formerly suggested by various touches that it was only one floor down from a fully-functioning studio. This effect was absent now, and what Honeybath surveyed was a big and rather expensively furnished room of a neutral and uninteresting sort. Since the Lightfoots, whatever else was to be said of them, were neither of them personalities of the most conforming order, there was thus a kind of uneasy hiatus between themselves and their surroundings. They had lived here for a long time, but one felt them to be now perched in the place without attachment to it—a fact uncomfortably suggesting that they had ceased to feel much attachment to one another. Moreover there was a good deal of dust and even cobweb around, and in a large Chinese jar in a window embrasure Melissa had created a somewhat aggressive arrangement of hothouse flowers which had now been in evident decline for many days. This last appearance depressed Honeybath a good deal. Dead flowers in a dwelling over which a woman presides are a signal which it doesn't require a psychiatrist to interpret.

Lightfoot was having trouble with the flannel. The stuff had been cut into long slips, and had to be coped with in the manner of the puttees that Honeybath recalled having to wear when in the O.T.C. at his public school. It seemed clear that Flannel Foot, or Vickers, had been a veridical and not a merely legendary burglar; but that he had encumbered himself in this grotesque fashion in the interest of achieving a cat-like tread seemed hard to believe. It was just the thing, however, to catch Edwin's fancy. Honeybath suddenly remembered an occasion upon which his friend had declared himself to be a reincarnation of Katsushika Hokusai, provided himself with a becoming kimono, and executed some very colourable pastiches of popular things like *The Hollow of the Deep-Sea Wave*. That had been genuine and innocent clowning of an artist's kind that they had both enjoyed together. But this burglar-impersonation, apparently prompted by the discovery that Lightfoot kept the courts where Flannel Foot had gloried and drunk deep (supposing the late Mr Vickers to have been of intemperate habit) had something genuinely dotty to it. And Edwin had once been the painter he had been! Honeybath was much perturbed by the present state of the case. What Edwin had been was something that he himself could never be. But he had been Edwin's friend, and it was now up to him to establish himself again as that. In fact it was his duty to sort Edwin out. Honeybath wondered whether the first step must be to give a good shake such as would disentangle Edwin from his idiotic wife. It was a dangerous thought, with something jealous and possessive lurking at the heart of it. Honeybath, being a perceptive person, was dimly aware of this. He was even prompted to withdraw and leave things

as they were. But as the evening developed, the impulse to
do something grew on him.

Strangely enough, what was operative here was the instinct
of a gentleman and a feeling of duty as much towards the
tedious Melissa as towards the lost genius she had married.
The Leoville-Poyferre (which turned out to be 1966, an out-
standing year) did Lightfoot no good. The bottle had been
produced and uncorked with proper care—and then its
proprietor declared it wasn't what he wanted to drink.
What he wanted to drink was malt whisky, and the only
malt whisky fit to offer his old friend was 'that stuff from
Islay'. Honeybath remembered what this obscure island
produced; it had a peaty tang to it that was incomparable
without a doubt. Moreover the hour for just such a species
of delectation was appropriate enough. But this didn't
condone the turn Lightfoot now put on. Not that it was a
turn; it was involuntary and compulsive in a most disturbing
way. Lightfoot pottered here and there in quest of the desired elixir; he seemed resolved to turn the whole flat upside
down; minute by minute his agitation increased; he ended
up in a phrenetic condition such as no woman should be
expected to live with. And Melissa didn't suffer it with the
patience which alone might have tided things over. She
screamed at her husband to let up and sit down. Honeybath
had to face the fact that the domestic life of the Lightfoots
was a shambles.

Yet there was still a great deal of enchantment about
Edwin. In the middle of this ridiculous and demeaning
brouhaha he would say things that could come only from
an angel. Or from an archangel ruined—Honeybath thought,
groping after some obscure literary allusion. Eventually they
resigned themselves to the claret, and also to the loss of
Melissa's society, since she took herself off in a graceless if
very understandable fashion to another room. For a short

space of time this disappearance seemed significantly to relieve Edwin's tensions and tantrums; he talked about contemporary painters from Rothko to Hockney in a manner showing that he still kept his eye effectively on the professional ball. But on a third glass of claret this faded out. Edwin began not to talk but to mumble. He mumbled about Edwin, and about Edwin alone. Life had given, and was giving, Edwin Lightfoot a raw deal. For an hour Honeybath listened, or failed to listen, to the resentments and obsessions of a grown man who was regressing to the condition of a frustrated and self-absorbed child. This was bad enough. Worse was the character of the glance that Edwin occasionally directed at him. It was the glance of a grown man who knew where he had arrived and was mutely begging that some life-line be thrown to him.

Or so it seemed to Charles Honeybath. The curious thought came to him that it was a case of regression going rather too far. He knew almost nothing about his friend's childhood—except that it wasn't to be regretted if one took the larger view. Whatever had wounded him then had armed him in his prime. *Mighty poets are cradled forth in wrong. They learn in suffering what they teach in song.* Shelley had said something like that. And Edwin had now simply moved back too far. If one could have started him off on a well-controlled time-machine, and then shunted him backwards only to the point at which his genius was in flower. . . .

Charles Honeybath was a sensible man, and this bizarre and vain idea naturally didn't linger in his mind. He turned to consider what practical steps he could take to rescue Edwin from his present impasse. He had gained the impression that his friend hardly ever went out; he lived cooped up in this damned flat—and if he amused himself there it was by pretending to be some small-time crook who either had or had not been his predecessor as its proprietor. It was a state of affairs too grotesque and painful to be thought of. Couldn't Edwin be got away, even if only now and then? Honeybath, although not a particularly sociable man, moved among his fellow-artists to a reasonable extent. There were plenty of informal groups—coteries and dining-clubs—where Edwin Lightfoot would be welcomed without question as the great painter he was or had been. Could Edwin be enticed into such company? Honeybath asked himself the question, and faced the fact that it must probably be answered in the negative. Edwin felt himself to be a failure, and to be far too old for any sort of effective come-back. He simply wouldn't want to meet his peers.

But *festina lente*. Here wasn't a situation to rush. The important thing was to establish that this attempt at reunion hadn't been a fiasco; that there had been pleasure in it, and that it would happen again. In this interest Honeybath from time to time said what he could in a sympathizing and concerned way to the man hunched in a chair before him; and it was after midnight when he took his leave. Edwin hardly stirred, but there was again just that ghost of an appealing look. Honeybath would almost have preferred the air of factitious amusement which Edwin had contrived when hard at work being Flannel Foot.

At the front door, and as he was letting himself out, he was intercepted, to his surprise, by Melissa. Melissa was carrying a rather dusty suitcase in the direction of what he recalled as her bedroom. She set it down with a bump.

'Well,' Melissa said. 'He knows now. The old friend turns up at the eleventh hour—or just after the twelfth, as it happens—and learns all.'

'Melissa,' Honeybath said, 'I'm afraid things aren't going too happily with Edwin—or with yourself, either.'

'And he has a wonderful sense of just what's happening. Although not, perhaps, in my room.'

'In your room, Melissa?'

'It's still that at the moment, but it won't be tomorrow. I'm packing.' Melissa gave a shrill laugh. 'I'm going home to mother.'

'But surely your mother . . .'

'The man's a fool. Of course she died years ago. I'm going off with a lover. Or perhaps I shall just buy a parrot. A parrot would be safer, on the whole.'

'Melissa, surely you should consider . . .'

'Before he starts preaching he ought to try living with him. When the enterprising burglar's not a-burgling he's hard at work boring his wife to death. Charles, goodbye.'

With this quite irregular departure into direct address Mrs Lightfoot picked up the suitcase again and vanished into her room.

III

ON THE DAY following his pilgrimage to Holland Park Charles Honeybath stepped off a perfectly familiar kerb, appeared to trip over his own feet, fell, and broke a wrist. The accident upset him figuratively as well as literally. For a short time he suffered excruciating pain, and for a much longer time had to put up with considerable inconvenience, since the surgeons had for some reason decided to make quite heavy weather of what was surely a minor mishap. But the underlying reason for Honeybath's being much disturbed was (as he perfectly well knew) that he belonged to a generation one of whose sacred books had been *The Psychopathology of Everyday Life*. It would be absurd, he believed, to regard his friend the pianist's accident as having been an *accident*; the poor man had seen his finger sliced off (and actually hurled into a gooseberry bush) because his earliest ambition had been to achieve distinction as an engine-driver, so that his deeper mind regarded banging away on a musical instrument as constituting a humiliating second-best. Honeybath had renewed his acquaintance with Edwin Lightfoot, decidedly *il miglior fabbro*, even if it was now as *un fabbro maledetto* (or at least *avariato*) that one would have to describe him. So Honeybath's genius had been rebuked, with the result that he never wanted to face an easel again, and had incapacitated himself accordingly. The fact that it was his left wrist and not his right that he had contrived to incapacitate did a little complicate the diagnosis.

But a loss of nerve is a loss of nerve. And this was why Honeybath decided to make sure of his ground at Hanwell Court.

Hanwell Court was to be his haven: the secure (and rather stately) harbour to which he was to retreat when, in five, or ten—or even fifteen?—years' time, he was no longer up to facing the buffeting waves of Chelsea life. Hanwell Court was much sought after by the superior orders of society with this sort of end in view, and he had already put down a substantial deposit to ensure his place in the queue. But he was not without misgivings about it. Would it prove to be what Henry James had thought of as the Great Good Place, or would it turn out to be a well-upholstered funk-hole of a depressing sort? The inmates—an ironically-tinged word it rather pleased him to have thought of, and which he regularly used when speaking of his intention to his friends—might turn out to be not, so to speak, his sort of inmates. They might walk across the park to church in a species of crocodile every Sunday. They might read detective stories or even 'romantic' fiction; they might treat as a pariah one who shirked his duty at the bridge table. He had of course cased the joint; been shown over it by a commanding female whom he had misdoubtfully suspected ought to be addressed as 'Matron'. But the actual inmates had been little on view. It had been explained to him that this was on account of their all commanding their own spacious quarters, from which they emerged only to lunch or dine, or as they pleased. At Hanwell Court you were securely elevated above the miserable world of bed-sitters and shared 'facilities'. You could have your private life, just as you had your private privy.

On the whole it had seemed satisfactory enough, and Honeybath wasn't altogether clear why he had suddenly decided to take another look at the place. It wasn't merely because of his tumble, and reflection suggested to him that the Lightfoots had something to do with it. Here were two very old friends, or at least a very old friend and his wife, approaching with a painful obviousness the end of a road. Perhaps they could be regarded as a special case—being both, as they were, more than a little dotty. But in old age who wasn't liable to turn that way? Perhaps Honeybath himself was, without noticing it, teetering on the verge. Didn't he ceaselessly talk aloud as he drove through the countryside in the solitude of his car? Didn't he sometimes make grotesque faces at himself in his shaving-mirror for no reason at all? Didn't he hunch himself up in bed in an infantile and indeed foetal position when it would really be more comfortable, as well as dignified, to lie stretched out like a statue on a tomb? Nothing of all this seemed directly connected with Edwin and Melissa; yet there was no doubt that the spectacle of life getting out of hand with them was distressing and shaking him very much. And this was so even although he had seen neither of them again. His misadventure on the kerb had prevented his making any speedy return to the flat in Royal Crescent, and in addition to this he felt there might be something intrusive in seeming to elevate into a crisis that business of Melissa's declaring she was clearing out. Perhaps it was a threat she made every week, and what he had blown in on was no more than a recurrent tiff such as married couples commonly indulge in harmlessly enough.

The domestic relations of the Lightfoots nagged at him, all the same. He even felt that if—what he didn't at all intend—he made his retreat into Hanwell Court at once, he might come to feel that he had withdrawn from a fray in which his friends were still honourably engaged : by the 'fray' being meant simply carrying on with one's habitual manner of life even when it turned sticky in one way or another.

When he did return to Royal Crescent it was in a mid-afternoon, and again unheralded. He went in a cab, since he had provided himself with a rather large bouquet—the sort of thing small girls or boys hand to the Queen—and he had felt this might mildly embarrass him on a bus. He had remembered Melissa's neglected flowers, and vaguely felt that a good dollop of fresh-cut ones might cheer her up.

There proved, however, to be no Melissa to hearten— and no Edwin either. There was nothing but a furniture van, and a number of burly men huddling the Lightfoots' possessions into it. Alarmed and seeking information, Honeybath squeezed past these sweating persons and penetrated to the flat. The directing intelligence of the operation proved to be a man even more burly than the others, and enjoying as a consequence the character of a foreman. He regarded Honeybath with suspicion (quite massively and elaborately, since he had nothing else to do), and professed entire ignorance of anything except the immediate job in hand. It was his business to see the flat cleared of everything that could be removed or wrenched from its place, and then dumped in something he called the depository. One or two of the other men looked at Honeybath rather hopefully. There being no proprietors of the flat in evidence, he represented their only chance of any additional remuneration for their day's labour. Nothing of the kind came into Honeybath's head, and he was about to withdraw from this melancholy and disconcerting scene when a fresh arrival a little changed the situation. This was none other than a certain Mrs Plover, whom Honeybath dimly remembered from long ago as a lady occasionally obliging the Lightfoots in a cleaning and polishing way. As things now were, she appeared to enjoy the status of an old retainer, and it looked as if she had accepted the task of a final tidy up when the removal men had done their worst. Honeybath, although he was extremely perturbed by the whole affair (and hurt in his mind as well), at once greeted her with firm cordiality.

'My dear Mrs Plover,' he said, 'this is very strange. I had no idea of it. I've been a little out of touch with the Lightfoots of late. Where have they moved to?'

'I don't know as to 'er'. Mrs Plover spoke darkly. 'But Mr Ell, 'e gone orf to Italy.'

'Dear me! Well, it's a nice time of year for it.' Honeybath felt that a certain cover-up of his dismay was prudent.

'I never did 'old with Italians, Mr Haich. There was one next door to us when I was a kid. A mangy little monkey 'e went in for, wot sat on his 'urdy-gurdy. A narsty flea-bag, it was.' Mrs Plover's speech might have been described as vigorously demotic.

'Ah, yes—I remember that sort of thing. The monkey would be taught to hold a cap and collect pennies. But there have been some quite notable Italians in times past, Mrs Plover. Masaccio and Michelangelo, for example. And Piero della Francesca.' This pointless informativeness showed that Honeybath was in great confusion. 'Has Mr Lightfoot left a forwarding address?'

'Ten quid down to clear up the mess, and never a bloody 'int of his whereabouts.' Mrs Plover produced a soiled apron from a string bag. 'Not that Mr Ell mayn't be keeping on the studio, it seems. A dirty mucky place that I'm glad I never put 'and to. But a separate dwelling in the eye of the law.'

'No doubt. Well, I mustn't detain you from your work, Mrs Plover.' Honeybath's only thought at the moment was to get away from the distressing chaos around him, and think things out. 'But if you should hear from Mrs Lightfoot meanwhile . . .'

'I won't hear nuffink from 'er'. Mrs Plover was emphatic. 'But one thing I do know—and not to 'er credit. I was unsurprised. She said it would remind 'er of the charms of Mr Ell's conwersation.'

'Whatever was that, Mrs Plover?'

'What she gone and bought, of course. A bloody great parrot.'

Honeybath turned away and prepared to leave the flat. He disapproved of Melissa's parrot, Melissa's joke about it, and Mrs Plover's language. Halfway to the door he discovered that he was still carrying a large bunch of red and white carnations dolled up with fluffy fern and swathed in tissue paper and silver foil. He could hardly drop this ridiculous burden on the floor, and to hand it to one of the burly men might be an action carrying the most sinister implications. So he came back and handed it to Mrs Plover instead.

'I wonder if you would care to have these?' he asked. 'I should like you to have them. It's possible we mayn't meet again.'

'I'll be 'appy, Mr Haich,' Mrs Plover said. And she looked, oddly enough, quite as gratified as surprised.

On this note of amenity Honeybath got out of the flat—which it appeared likely that he was saying goodbye to too. On the landing he paused, conscious of a sudden strong curiosity about the state of the big studio on the top floor. It was, of course, very familiar to him, and now there came into his mind one immediately relevant fact. As a precaution against inconvenience arising from his own absent-mindedness, Edwin never brought away the key when he locked the place up behind him. He simply shoved it under the terminal few inches of the stair-carpet. So far as Honeybath knew, there had never been any ill-consequence of this guileless notion of security (of which the authentic Flannel Foot would certainly have thought poorly). But it did make it quite probable that Honeybath could pay a quiet visit to the studio before leaving the building. As he saw it, there would be nothing improper in this. He and Edwin had been on terms that amply licensed anything of the sort, and there was no reason to maintain that they were not on the same terms still.

He mounted the final flight of stairs doubtfully, all the same. The burly men were clustered round Melissa's grand piano on a lower landing, and their language cast the mild impropriety of Mrs Plover's in the shade. It would be awkward, however, if one of them looked up and shouted at him. Fortunately this didn't happen, and the key was in its familiar hiding-place. Honeybath unlocked the door of the studio and went in.

It was a single very large room under the roof—into which there had been inset a large skylight. Off it there opened two small and low-hutched dens which appeared long ago to have served as rudimentary kitchen and yet more rudimentary bathroom. (Perhaps the late burglarious Mr Vickers, if he had indeed lived here, had let it out to some *confrère* less eminent in the profession.) These ancillary accommodations no doubt made it possible to envisage living in the place as well as painting in it. And this seemed indeed to be in the absent Edwin Lightfoot's mind. The sole marked change in the studio since Honeybath had seen it last was the introduction of a brand-new single bed. It hadn't occurred to Lightfoot, planning some alteration in his manner of life, to introduce an unobtrusive object of similar utility called a 'studio couch' or something of the sort. Or, if it had, he had nevertheless decided upon this more bleakly assertive measure. Married life—the narrow bed declared—had packed up on him. And in this Bohemian

fashion he was going to set up his abode when he returned
from Italy.

Honeybath approved of Italy; it was a distressed painter's
obvious resource. He didn't approve of the proposal to pig
in the studio. It would be all right for a young man. And
there were, perhaps, older men for whom it would be all
right too. But it just wasn't Edwin. Honeybath was wholly
clear about this. It was part of the atrophy (as it must
brutally be called) of his friend's genius that he had turned
rather self-indulgent in the most commonplace ways. And
Melissa, who had more than a streak of domestic competence when she was feeling like it, had always done him
fairly well—or had done so until the recent phase of
strained relations. Edwin's ability to do for himself would
have been minimal at the best of times, since he simply
wasn't a practical man. In the plan he appeared to have
formed there was no future whatever.

But the studio, when Honeybath walked round it, bore
at least the superficial appearance of being in full working
order. And the smell, too, was right; it was like that of a
good sauce of the more complex sort, the diverse ingredients
of which are still at play upon one another and have not yet
faded into an inert continuum. There was even token of a
work in progress, since a fairly large canvas was disposed
on the easel, covered with a light cloth. Honeybath respected
its reclusion, since he was a punctilious man, but otherwise
poked freely about. A good many completed paintings were
in evidence, unframed, and stacked up one against another,
face to the wall. It was a state of affairs reminding him of
the earliest phase of his own career; these works were in a
kind of queue, he supposed, awaiting exposure in discreet
numbers in some dealer's gallery—probably Ambrose
Prout's. Honeybath examined a few at random, and didn't
greatly care for what he found. They were landscapes of

undoubted technical mastery, but repetitive and almost formulaic, as if the artist had long ago compounded for a limited number of schemata which were more and more peeping through the varied compositions based upon them. It was sad, but true, that there was very little fire to Edwin Lightfoot nowadays. What that failed painter and prolific writer William Hazlitt had been fond of calling *gusto* had evaporated from his work.

Everything, Honeybath noticed, was conscientiously dated as well as signed. This even applied to a number of minor efforts, all recent, of quite a different sort : rapidly executed portrait-sketches in pencil on wet paper, some of women but for the most part of men. About these there was sometimes something tentative and alert, as if Edwin had been waking up to the necessity of breaking new ground. It was, in a sense, Honeybath's own ground. When an Oxford or Cambridge college, or a City livery company wrote to Honeybath stating that they had it in mind to 'procure a likeness' of this worthy or that there was something very satisfactory in the slightly archaic expression. Honeybath liked trying to produce a likeness, and he was rather touched to find Edwin engaged in tentative essays at the same thing. He was even glad to acknowledge that these deft scribbles and smudges held something of the true Lightfoot—the true Lightfoot being (according to Honeybath's own loyal definition) one who had a little something that Honeybath hadn't got. Here and there, for example, there were evident bold accentuations partaking of the nature of *caricatura*, so that the 'likeness' was at once of the man anybody could see and of the same man's ideal form as it might exist laid up in heaven. But many of these sketches, even when plainly felicitous, had been crumpled up or torn in two. This was the only evidence of a disturbed, as distinct from an exhausted, Edwin Lightfoot visible in the studio.

In the end Honeybath left the abandoned room, and made his way downstairs past the empty flat, himself a little more disturbed than when he had arrived. It was up to him, he again felt, to mount some sort of rescue operation on Edwin's behalf. He recalled with grave distaste the nonsense of his friend's recent 'charade'. Hadn't there been something perverse or wanton in it rather than truly mad? And didn't these sketches suggest an Edwin who was struggling to regain contact with folk in all their stimulating diversity, and who realized that he had been living in an injudicious near-solitude, with little company except Melissa and the ghost of a burglar?

These thoughts were still in Honeybath's head on the following morning, when he boarded a train at Paddington with the object of taking that second look at Hanwell Court which was to clarify, he hoped, the vexed problem of his own later course of life.

IV

HE HAD BECOME—Honeybath told himself—something of a creature of habit: a state of affairs which the approach of old age doubtless regularly promotes. Why else had he bought himself a first-class ticket? Since few people now travelled by British Rail except at other people's expense, one very commonly found the Firsts more crowded than the Seconds. One was apt, in fact, to find oneself seated between two business men (or 'businessm'n', as the B.B.C. now liked to call them) and with three persons in a similar walk of life facing one. When neither asleep nor shamelessly perusing girlie magazines, they were usually annotating sheafs of repellent-looking typescript, or doing endless sums on miniature calculating machines, or drooling unceasingly into pocket tape-recorders. On this occasion, however, it looked as if he was to have a compartment to himself—a portent, perhaps, of the near-paralysis which he understood to be invading the industrial and commercial life of the country. He settled himself comfortably in a corner; placed on the seat beside him his hat, his gloves, and the handsomely illustrated brochure uttered by the proprietors of Hanwell Court to their prospective clients (or inmates). He then opened a copy of the *Burlington Magazine*.

Just before the train drew out of the station, however, the door giving on the corridor was drawn back, and an elderly man cast an appraising glance over the available accommodation. Satisfied with the *Lebensraum* on offer, he made an entry somewhat impeded by the necessity of manipulating through the door a substantial and seemingly over-weighted suitcase. Honeybath put down his magazine and made courteous gestures indicative of his willingness to assist. Between them they dumped the suitcase on a seat, since it was much too heavy to hoist to the luggage-rack overhead. Its proprietor expressed his thanks with a well-bred absence of effusion. Honeybath withdrew into his magazine. The train's first stop was to be at Didcot. So he could enjoy a long comfortable read of matter well calculated to elevate his mind above the personal concerns motivating his journey.

He didn't look up until the train was hurtling through Ealing Broadway. What he then saw startled him considerably. His fellow-traveller had opened the suitcase, which could be glimpsed as containing a variety of gleaming metallic objects not immediately to be identified. But from among these had evidently come something that the elderly man was now gripping firmly in his mouth. It was a slender dagger of the most sinister appearance. And the muscular effort required for this unnerving performance had the effect of contorting his features into a ferocious *rictus* the impact of which was momentarily enhanced by a glance that could be described only as wild and glaring.

Honeybath wasn't the less alarmed through his having seen something of the sort before. There are Japanese actor prints in which ferocious persons thus exhibit themselves as literally armed to the teeth. But this didn't at all explain the appearance of a similar phenomenon in an English railway-carriage.

'I do beg your pardon.' The elderly man, who had necessarily unmouthed the dagger to achieve this articulateness, smiled disarmingly. 'And I wonder whether you are interested, sir, in this kind of thing? Yesterday, I am delighted to say, I made a most successful raid on Sotheby's.'

'A raid?' It was with a natural alarm that Honeybath repeated the word.

'One of my regular forays, my dear sir. Once or twice I may have bid a shade injudiciously. But I was well satisfied in the end.'

'I am delighted to hear it. Did your purchases include that—um—poniard?'

'*Panzerbrecher*—if you will forgive the correction. But indeed yes. I have been looking out for one for a long time. Its use, as you know, was to penetrate the joints of the armour of an unhorsed opponent. It thus belongs to the general category of the *misérecorde*, the name by which is denominated any weapon designed to administer the *coup de grâce*—or, alternatively, to thrust sufficiently far and painfully into an adversary's person to educe a plea for mercy. But my chief prize yesterday was a more complex weapon of the same sort, at one time much in use by the emissaries of the Fehmic Courts—or the *Vehmgerichte*, which you will recall as the uncorrupted term. And here it is.' The elderly man rummaged in his suitcase and produced another small dagger. 'It had, of course, the same function. Only here is a spring one may release with the thumb. Pray watch the blade.'

Honeybath watched the blade, although without enthusiasm. He saw it instantly transform itself into three more slender blades disposed as on a fork or trident.

'The significance is, as you will have realized, religious,' the elderly man said with mild satisfaction. 'Execution has been carried out in the name of the Holy Trinity. May I venture to inform you that my name is Richard Gaunt? I have a reason for so presuming.'

'I am Charles Honeybath.' Honeybath didn't commonly exchange such information with persons casually encountered in public conveyances. But his interlocutor, if slightly odd, was demonstrably a man of impeccable comportment and address. 'How do you do?' he added, stretching a further point.

'How do you do? My excuse for hazarding so irregular a mode of introduction, Mr Honeybath, is to be found in the brochure I see lying beside you. I infer from it that you have some interest in Hanwell Court. I am on my way there now. It has been my home for several years.'

'I am most interested to hear it.' Honeybath eyed with genuine curiosity the first inmate of his proposed haven with whom he had achieved speaking terms. 'And you keep your collection there?'

'Yes, indeed. Collecting is quite a thing with a number of us. Lady Munden, for example, collects seaweed. Indeed, she may be said to cultivate seaweed, if that is the term. She is not without hope of achieving some notable hybridities.'

'I should suppose that to be difficult, so far from the sea?'

'The establishment has provided Lady Munden with a large saline pool. It is always very good in that sort of way. But, between you and me, it seems probable that medical considerations were involved. The contemplation of seaweed would appear to have a composing effect upon the emotions.'

'I see.' Honeybath wondered whether the same was to be said of the contemplation of outlandish weaponry. To this occupation, indeed, Mr Gaunt was now showing a disposition to return. He was rummaging in the suitcase.

'Now, I wonder,' he said, 'whether I have anything else that might interest you? Ah! Here is the hopper for my Gatling gun. It is the last piece missing, so I believe I can now assemble the thing. Not from Sotheby's, this; I picked it up in a useful little place I know of in the Mile End Road. A remarkable achievement in its day, the Gatling gun. It has justly been commemorated in the poetical sphere.

> *We have got*
> *The Gatling gun, and they have not.*

Kipling, no doubt.'

'Belloc, more probably.' Honeybath cast a dubious eye over what was now being exhibited to him. 'Your interest in your subject appears to be wide-ranging,' he said. 'Does it stretch to practical ballistics? When you have put together this Gatling-thing will you get round to firing it?'

'Oh, very probably—very probably indeed. There is Colonel Dacre's rifle-range, you know. They constructed it for him after the accident to Admiral Emery. There is a great deal of forethought at Hanwell.'

'I am delighted to hear it.' Honeybath hesitated upon this. He rather regretted having exposed the promotional material for Hanwell Court on the seat beside him. Had he not done so, indeed, he would have failed to pick up some interesting scraps of information on the place from this harmless connoisseur of violence. But now he could not very well conceal the purpose of his present journey. It wouldn't do, for instance, to say that he was proposing to inspect Hanwell Court as a possible place of residence for a maiden aunt, or something of that sort. It looked as if he and Mr Gaunt were going to arrive there together, and if this happened any prevarication would almost certainly be detected. But then why think in terms of 'detection' at all? He saw that at heart he must be a little ashamed of the whole project—almost as if he were thinking in terms of being sent to gaol or entering a home for alcoholics. This was very absurd—but there it was. Perhaps like Othello he had an instinct for an unhoused free condition, and if he settled for Hanwell would come to regret its circumscription and confine.

'I'm booked into Hanwell Court myself,' he said, suddenly

and firmly. 'At least in a tentative way. And I'm running down to take another look at it.'

'Excellent, Mr Honeybath! I sincerely hope you don't think better of your resolve. I shall look forward to many pleasant confabulations over this joint interest of ours. Daggers and stilettos make a large and intricate study in themselves, do they not? Have you ever thought, by the way, of specializing in those that came to be employed in duelling? Do you run to a *main gauche*?'

'I haven't even heard of it. And you are mistaken, Mr Gaunt, in supposing that I . . .'

'It was, of course, named from the fact that it was held in the left hand and used for parrying. I lately acquired a specimen with a toothed edge on which the adversary's sword could be caught and broken. But in the main, I confess, I have of late been working mainly in the field of offensive weapons. Hyper-offensive weapons, indeed, if the term is an admissible one. They exert a peculiar fascination over me. The dagger with the poison-channel, as perfected in Mantua : there is great scope there. And the amazing ingenuity so often employed in inventing blades capable of inflicting particularly awkward lacerations. I have read that the poet Browning was an enthusiastic devotee of these.'

Honeybath felt disposed to say, 'But the painter Honeybath is not.' He reflected, however, that this might be (at least metaphorically) wounding, and that Mr Gaunt's hobbyhorse was entirely innocent. Moreover, it looked as if they might be destined at least to pass the time of day for the remainder of their joint lives. So he held his peace while being shown several more lethal objects which had been knocked down to his companion the day before. The total sum of money that had thereby passed through Messrs Sotheby's hands must have been very considerable. But then Hanwell Court was far from being any refuge for genteel

indigence. What it *was* a refuge for, Honeybath was beginning to feel he hadn't been quite adequately informed. Was
Colonel Dacre more careless than a military man ought to
be of the conditions under which he fired off his rifle? Had
Admiral Emery perished on the instant, like poor Admiral
Byng on his quarter-deck at Portsmouth? Was Lady Munden
really provided with lavish facilities for treating bits of seaweed as if they were dahlias or sweet peas? Was his new
acquaintance Mr Gaunt any more to be trusted with fire-
arms (or even *misérecordes* and *mains gauches*) than his
fellow-inmate the colonel? Honeybath decided to seek
cautious enlightenment on these matters. So in a pause
after Mr Gaunt had finished expounding the operation of
something called a *bouche à feu* he ventured on a change
of subject.

'Would it be impertinent,' he asked, 'to inquire what
directed your interest to Hanwell Court in the first place?'

'Ah, that was a matter of my trustees.' Mr Gaunt was
clearly not offended. 'For some years I have found it con-
venient to have my financial affairs, and so forth, conducted
by persons of that sort. And I am fortunate enough to have
very reliable trustees. After comparing notes with a number
of our residents I have come to the conclusion that I am
very fortunate indeed. By no means all are as satisfied as I
am.'

'I am sorry to hear that. Troublesome trustees must be
extremely vexatious.' Honeybath paused on this sympathetic
note. 'Lady Munden, for example,' he said at a venture.
'Does she not get on too well with hers?'

'She is far from pleased with them. I think I may say—
strictly in confidence, Mr Honeybath—that the seaweed
has to be described as an inexpensive second-best. Lady
Munden had formed the project, the wholly laudable project, of purchasing a substantial stretch of the park at

Hanwell and constituting it a reserve for threatened indigen-
ous fauna. She was simply told that the money wasn't there.'
Mr Gaunt shook his head in a sombre fashion. 'Incredible
as it may seem, that is what her trustees told her. She then
offered to throw the enterprise open to the public for an
appropriate fee, and declared herself willing to sit in person
at a turnstile and collect the cash. She had made the most
careful calculations, she was able to declare, and was assured
there would be a substantial profit. But her trustees remained obdurate. These are grim times, Mr Honeybath,
grim times indeed. The late Sir Adrian Munden, although
not a man of good family, fell little short of being what you
and I would call a nabob. But here was plain penury
confronting his widow.'

'How very shocking.' Honeybath, who had perfected a
technique of offering composing remarks to tiresome sitters
for whom the times were out of joint, offered this absurd
untruth unblushingly. But the train was now slowing down
to make its first halt at Didcot, and he felt a strong impulse
to gather together his belongings and make a dash for freedom. But he reflected that Mr Gaunt's was possibly only a
partial view of society at Hanwell Court; that he belonged,
as it might be brutally put, to a lunatic fringe of the place.
Honeybath was, moreover, a man commendably curious
about his fellow-mortals in their inexhaustible variety, and
he told himself it was extravagant to suppose that by merely
venturing once more within the curtilage of Hanwell he
would put himself in any danger of being locked up. He
resolved to see the day's venture through.

'Ah, Didcot!' he said. 'An uninspiring gateway to the
Berkshire Downs, is it not? But I believe ours is the next
stop.'

'It is, indeed. May I ask, Mr Honeybath, if *you* have
good trustees?'

'I have not, as it happens, had any occasion to consider the point so far.' Honeybath offered this slightly evasive reply on a note of sudden gloom. Everybody ends up, he supposed, by being bossed around. Or everybody whose condition is such that there is money to be had out of the bossing. 'May I offer you my *Burlington Magazine*?' he asked. 'I notice an interesting article on what is to be gathered of the later history of armour from Gervase Markham's *Souldier's Accidence*.'

'Thank you. Thank you very much,' Mr Gaunt said politely. 'It is a subject a little aside from my own field of research. But it is always wise to broaden one's view.'

And Mr Gaunt, blessedly, absorbed himself in a purely defensive scene of things for the rest of the journey.

V

THE TRAVELLER WHO approaches Hanwell Court
by the main drive has the advantage of first viewing the
mansion disposed beyond a gigantic *repoussoir* known to art
historians as the *Poseidon urging the Sea-Monster to attack
Laomedon*. The monster has three heads, each with gaping
jaws, and these must have spewed water once upon a time,
since the whole group is perched within an enormous scallop
shell which must have served as the basin of the fountain
when it was a fountain in its native Italy. The entire
ensemble is now perched on a squat pedestal some twelve
feet high. The god straddles the monster, with arms flung
up in the conventional pose of a huntsman unleashing hounds.
Viewed from the rear (for the statue faces the house lying
in a shallow valley beyond) the uninstructed might conjecture that Poseidon is in fact his brother Zeus, and that
the business on hand is the directing of a thunderbolt against
some race of overweening mortals in the magnificent
architectural performance below.

Honeybath's brochure contained the information that
Hanwell Court had been completed, as to its main part, in
the year 1702. What is immediately presented to the eye
contemplating the main façade is six very tall windows on
either side of a very tall front door. Above these are thirteen
windows apparently equally tall (and in fact, therefore,
rather taller), the middle one being a third as broad as the
others. And above these again are thirteen squat little

46

windows beneath an oppressive cornice and an elegant balustrade. A visiting Martian might suppose the entire edifice designed for the occupation of a dozen or so giants who had enslaved a local population of dwarfs now cowering in attic hutches when not performing the menial duties required of them. And indeed the architect had probably had in mind social dispositions not altogether remote from this fantasy.

So much for 1702. Slightly later generations had built on, in the same classical taste, sundry wings, pavilion, and the like, some of them free-standing except for sweeping connective colonnades, designed for the better conduct of balls and banquets or the large-scale cultivation of exotic plants. What the whole effect didn't at all suggest was the possibility of tucking away in the interior adequately congruous but necessarily miniaturized accommodation for some two score of affluent persons resolved to carry gracious living along with them to the grave. Much of the original set-up must have been gutted and rebuilt in the interest of this intrepid proposal.

Honeybath drove up, still accompanied by the inmate Gaunt, in a conveyance which had been waiting for them in the station yard. He wondered whether he would be charged for this trip in a Rolls-Royce, or whether it would prove to be on the house. They had, after all, a good deal of his money already, and it must be earning interest for somebody. It was even possible that, in an indirect way, he had contributed to the cost of Lady Munden's saline pool and Colonel Dacre's rifle-range. These were doubtless unworthy thoughts, such as well-affected inmates would scorn to entertain. Not for the first time, he felt that he had perhaps made a mistake about Hanwell Court. Had he been corrupted by the assumptions of that class of society many of whose choicest ornaments he had for some years been contributing generously-interpreted likenesses of to the walls of Burlington House? It was a sombre thought.

It was also a thought prompting Honeybath to defer for a little longer his renewed encounter with the management of the place. So on descending from the Rolls he murmured to Mr Gaunt that he was a little early for the appointment he had made, and that he proposed to fill in the time by taking a short stroll in the grounds. Whereupon Mr Gaunt, having expressed the hope of seeing his new acquaintance in permanent residence very soon, departed into the house, followed by the chauffeur lugging the weighty suitcase.

Perhaps because it was a remarkably fine spring day, the precincts and policies of Hanwell were less dispeopled than on the occasion of Honeybath's previous visit. In the first of the formal gardens immediately below the terrace a lady in the soft and flowing garments held to become old age was snipping expertly at some sort of small flowering shrub. She was kind enough to pause in this occupation and bow to Honeybath as he went past. Honeybath swept off his hat in proper form. It was probably the convention that the inmates acknowledged one another's existence upon every fleeting encounter, and the lady had at once observed that he was not the sort of man who comes in to wind the clocks. At the corner of the terrace itself another elderly lady was seated in a comfortable chair, engaged in making a water-colour sketch of a spray of early roses trained against the mellow masonry of the house. Salutations were again exchanged, and Honeybath wondered whether it would be proper for him to pause and offer some quasi-professional comment on the work of art in hand. He decided that this would be a liberty, and might even involve him in having to explain that the lady's impromptu interlocutor was nothing less than a Royal Academician. So he walked on. It seemed to be worth noting, he told himself, that both these appropriately occupied females seemed entirely sane. But as neither of them had uttered, there could be no positive certainty on the point.

He descended to a lawn which had been laid out as that sort of putting green which has a dozen holes scattered over it, each marked by a little tin flag. It was the kind of recreational resource which one frequently remarks in public parks. A spare, grey-haired man of military bearing was involved with it. Honeybath wondered whether this might be Colonel Dacre, more pacifically employed than was his wont. His bearing was conventional but his behaviour was a little out-of-the-way; he was moving from hole to hole, removing each little flag in turn, kneeling down, and peering into the small cavity thus revealed. From this mysterious activity he abruptly desisted on marking Honeybath's approach.

'Good morning to you,' he said commandingly. 'Are you the man from the Patent Office?'

'No, sir, I am not.' Honeybath was considerably surprised by this unexpected question. 'I have no connection whatever with such an institution.'

'Ah! Well, I wrote to the Patent Office more than a week ago, and have been expecting them to send a fellow down.'

'Indeed, sir. I fear the only sort of fellow I am is an Honorary Fellow of my old Cambridge college.' Honeybath made this slightly unsuitable communication with some asperity. To be classed as a fellow was much the same thing as being expected to wind clocks. 'I regret,' he added, 'cheating your expectation in the matter.'

'It may be just as well. I am not sure that an application to the Patent Office hasn't been a mistake at this stage. I understand them to guarantee confidentiality, but one can never be certain of these things nowadays. There is a lot one can never be certain of. The increased use of plastics, for example. You know how these holes are constructed?'

'I can't say that I do.'

'The hole is punched out with the kind of affair one uses to plant daffodils and so forth. Then a small receptacle is inserted, the lip of which lies just below the level of the turf. It has to be fairly heavy, in order that a socket in its base may be capable of supporting the flag. You follow me?'

'Perfectly, sir.'

'I have taken it for granted, therefore, that these receptacles are invariably made of iron or steel. But the horrid thought has occurred to me that plastics may be coming in. I am relieved to find that it is not so. If, that is to say, one may go by the layout here. Plastic, you must understand, would entirely defeat my design. Observe this ball.' The military man suddenly held up a golf-ball. 'It is nothing less, sir, than a guided missile. It embodies a homing device. Or rather, it will shortly do so. There are one or two technical hitches, so far. The space available being so small, I am coming to think the mechanism will have to be transistorized. But the principle will be clear to you. Once you have reached the green, you may strike the ball with your putter pretty well in any direction you like. It will home on the hole, attracted by the only metallic object within its range, and simply drop into place.'

'I see.' Honeybath felt that he saw a good deal. He was in the presence of the Mad Scientist of popular fiction. 'Might it not be possible so to refine upon your device that success could infallibly be achieved straight from the tee? Golf has always seemed to me rather a slow affair. You are to be congratulated, sir, on an invention that will so notably speed up the game.'

'Precisely. But, of course, there are other possibilities.' The features of the inventor of the transistorized golf-ball suddenly transformed themselves into an expression of extreme cunning. 'Employed with restraint and discretion, my device would pretty well put the Open Championship within the grasp of any moderately competent player. It is conceivable that I may myself be that personage. The idea has attracted me since boyhood.'

Honeybath thought that this was probably true. He also thought that he had handled a potentially difficult situation with tolerable address. But this didn't mean that he wanted to spend his declining years humouring lunatics. If one was prepared to do that one could get paid for it as some sort of keeper or attendant in a madhouse. He wasn't yet clear that Hanwell Court was entirely, or even preponderantly, such a receptacle. It certainly sheltered a number of persons of markedly idiosyncratic tastes. But there was nothing very wrong with that. In the present age, when nearly everybody was being dismally pulped into a replica of everybody else, an institution standing up for oddity had much to commend it. Honeybath (who believed himself to be a stoutly unconventional type) wasn't going to come to premature conclusions. He bade the talented inventor of the homing golf-ball a cordial farewell, and walked on.

There was much that had to be judged entirely agreeable. The gardens were maintained in admirable order, and were so extensive and at the same time so variously secluded that any number of strollers could suppose themselves to be in solitary possession of the entire terrain. One could imagine the park to be one's own as well—and the house itself, for that matter, which every now and then appeared in one stately aspect or another as the various vistas on it opened up. This fictitious sense of ownership, although patently absurd, was surely innocent, and if one could pay for it among other amenities—well, why not? One can't extract such a feel from a 'luxury' hotel, and here it was on tap for approximately the same money.

Honeybath, although certain that he wouldn't care to

live permanently in this childish state of mind, found it amusing to luxuriate in for a few moments now. He was moving down the central path in an area somewhat formally conceived in the Italian taste, with high, square-clipped hedges on either hand, and here and there niches carved out of the foliage and framing miscellaneous stone urns, coffers, and blurred and eroded pieces of garden statuary. The vista, which was comparatively short, was closed by a well-proportioned little structure consisting of a circle of Ionic columns and a low domed roof. This frankly useless object, which would scarcely have afforded shade for a single garden chair, struck Honeybath as wholly pleasing, and he determined to walk on and round it before returning to the house. He had moved on a few yards, and was reflecting again on the ease with which solitude could be gained here, when he became aware that he wasn't in solitude after all. A figure had emerged from the scant shelter of the temple (or whatever it was conceived to be) and was now moving towards him. It was a man who could be distinguished as in middle age; and that he was attired with a somewhat obtrusive appropriateness to his rural situation could be inferred from his wearing (prematurely, as the season went) an immaculate Panama hat. Honeybath noted this, was conscious of the man hesitating for a moment, and then saw that he was again contemplating nothing but the natural scene—or the natural scene as straightened out, lopped, and elegantly adorned by human agency. The man in the Panama hat had vanished.

Since there appeared to be only unbroken and impenetrable walls of greenery on either hand between the temple and the spot where Honeybath stood, this was distinctly perplexing. The explanation appeared, however, when he had moved on a further dozen yards and discovered a narrow aperture in the hedge, indetectable until one was hard upon it. The man with the hat must have dodged quite rapidly through this. It wasn't Honeybath's business to follow and investigate. Nevertheless, he did so—merely because there lurked in him an impulse of juvenile curiosity which was always liable to bob up on sudden challenge. He walked through the gap, and confronted another hedge. He turned to his right, and yet a further hedge was before him; he turned again, and immediately realized what he had stumbled upon; he was in a cunningly designed and planted maze of a kind the best-known example of which in England is to be found at Hampton Court.

To seem to pursue a perfect stranger into the heart of such a contraption was highly unbecoming, and Honeybath at once endeavoured to beat a retreat. Unfortunately he moved in too rapid and unconsidered a fashion, with the result that he lost his bearings at the start, and was instantly as disorientated as if he were already half-way through the labyrinth. He took yet another turn, and found himself directly at gaze with the man in the Panama.

The situation was perhaps a little awkward, but ought not to have been actually embarrassing. Yet it was just that. For the man's attitude and expression rendered an impression of apprehensiveness and indeed alarm. And Honeybath had just registered this disconcerting fact when the man dodged aside—it was the only word for it—and once more vanished.

Honeybath wondered if the situation would be improved were he to call out a polite good morning. He had to judge that it would not. That he had actually pursued this in-offensive person into the maze was a fact impossible to disguise. He must simply continue his effort to emerge from the wretched thing, and trust that chance would not in the process produce a renewal of the rencounter.

But it may be called the general principle of a maze that

it is easier to get in than to get out. Honeybath turned
hither and thither, but to no avail. It was a curiously upsetting experience. He began to feel a little like a rat under
the invisible dispassionate gaze of some member of the
investigating classes—or if not this, at least a lobster in a pot.
He had to repress an irrational impulse to tear or claw
himself out of the place in a fashion that would have been
destructive to the whole device, ruinous to his attire, and
even scarifying to his person. He had just broken into a
blundering run, as if persuaded that mere impetus would
solve his problem, when a voice addressed him as from the
heavens above. He halted, looked upwards, and became
aware of a species of gazebo erected just beyond the perimeter of the maze. Only its upper platform was visible, and
on this the head and shoulders of the man addressing him.

'Easy, sir!' this person said soothingly and indulgently.
As he spoke he respectfully removed a cloth cap, a gesture
from which Honeybath inferred that this Ariadne-figure,
coming to the rescue, as it were, of her beloved Theseus, was
in fact a gardener. 'Would you be wanting still to get to the
centre?' this person went on, when apparently persuaded
that Honeybath was again reasonably composed. 'There's a
cage with some very pretty parakeets—very pretty indeed,
and well worth a visit.'

'Confound your parakeets!' Honeybath said, not very
civilly. 'I want to get out.'

'Then just turn round, sir, and do as I say.' The man on
the gazebo sounded a shade hurt in his mind. 'You're no
distance from the entrance, no distance at all. Straight on
until you can turn right, sir. That's it. Go on until you can
turn left. A nice morning for a stroll, wouldn't you say?
That's it! Left again now, and you might say freedom is
before you.'

In this somewhat ignominious way, Honeybath escaped from the maze, and found that Ariadne had descended from her perch and was awaiting him.

'Thank you very much,' he said. 'I'm afraid I was a little short with you about the birds. I've no doubt they are delightful. But I had no notion of threading the thing. My entering it at all was—um—inadvertent.'

'Just that, sir. And a maze is rather a flustering place.'

'No doubt.' Honeybath didn't enjoy being detected as having become flustered in so absurd a fashion. 'By the way, do you happen to have seen a man in a big white hat?'

'Ah, him! He's one of the shy ones, he is.' The gardener again spoke on his indulgent note. At the same time he looked at Honeybath appraisingly, as if estimating whether he was to be placed in the same category. 'Would you just have come into residence, as they say?'

'No, nothing of the kind. But I have an appointment at the house, and it looks as if I may be late for it.' Honeybath found he didn't want to prolong this humiliating episode. He wondered whether he ought to tip his rescuer. It was unlikely that the inmates of Hanwell Court went around handing out sums of money in return for small services, but his own position as a casual intruder was somewhat different. He decided that Ariadne would take no exception to the cost of a couple of pints, and acted accordingly. 'Thank you very much,' he said again. 'Perhaps I'll see the birds on another occasion. Meantime, good morning to you.'

As he walked away he found himself thinking not about the gardener but about the man in the Panama. Was he among those of the inmates whom a tactful meiosis would describe as disturbed? Curiously enough, he felt not. Although undoubtedly a shy one, he hadn't given the impression of being off his head. Rather, he had seemed rationally wary, much as a displaced person in an unfamiliar environment might be. This was a perplexing notion, and Honeybath didn't make a great deal of it. He walked on briskly, reached the front door of the house, rang a bell, and made himself known to the servant who answered it.

VI

THERE WAS A small hitch. Brigadier Luxmoore (who
was styled the Bursar, and was presumably the top man in
an administrative way at Hanwell Court) had been called
away on a family emergency, and had left Honeybath his
apologies. Dr Michaelis, however, was holding himself
available. Honeybath judged it legitimate to inquire what
position Dr Michaelis held in the establishment, and was told
that he was the Medical Superintendent. He had already
gathered from his brochure, and indeed from what he had
been told on his previous visit, that full medical and nursing
services were on tap at Hanwell. Even when terminal illness
befell you the place didn't turn you out except in your
coffin. But that it should actually support a resident physic-
ian seemed a shade disconcerting. If it didn't suggest a
madhouse (as at least some other evidences did), it at least
suggested a sanatorium. For some reason Honeybath at once
thought of the one in Thomas Mann's *The Magic Mountain*.
There was a Dr Krokowski there, who chatted you up on
your complexes when he wasn't tapping your chest. Perhaps
Dr Michaelis was a psychiatrist. It was more probable that
he simply went in for geriatrics in a general way. Honeybath wasn't attracted by the notion of becoming a subject
for the application of gerontology. He wasn't that old yet.
And he never wanted to be, either. Perhaps if he could read
his own future what would be revealed would be a merci-
fully instant encounter with a bus. But that wasn't to be

57

relied on—which was why he was poking around Hanwell Court now.

Dr Michaelis himself proved to be no greybeard. He was youngish, alert, and possessed of good professional manners. It was clear that he was accustomed to deal with more than medical issues when required, and that this familiarity extended to the behaviour of prospective clients cautiously obtruding second thoughts about closing with Hanwell Court. Honeybath noted with approval that he was far from pushing any objectionable sales-talk.

'It's entirely a matter of the times, isn't it?' Michaelis asked pleasantly. 'Formerly, an elderly woman of some substance would continue to live in her own house, with a reliable servant or two, and a companion. A man like yourself would do something very similar; he'd have a flat or chambers conveniently placed for his club, and so forth, and a reliable man who'd cook for him and valet him and everything else. But for decades now the whole trend of social legislation has militated against all that. We have to huddle together if we're to survive. That seems the long and the short of it. And here at Hanwell Court we try to provide the huddle without any positive squash. It's expensive, and it's going to become more so. But you've probably had the figures about all that.'

'Yes, I have,' Honeybath said. He was inclined to be favourably impressed by Michaelis's frank avowal of the state of the case.

'I suppose,' Michaelis went on, 'that most reasonably civilized people aren't too keen on gross inequalities of wealth. But downright levelling and crude egalitarianism are another matter. It's hard not to feel we're being specially pitched on, wouldn't you say, Mr Honeybath?'

'I don't know that I see it particularly that way.' Honeybath was slightly surprised by this drift in the Medical

Superintendent's conversation. 'Some are being impoverished more quickly than others, no doubt. But pretty well everybody is in for a bad time.'

'Don't you ever have a sense that unknown people—faceless men, as it has been very well put—are ganging up against you? That you must almost regard yourself as the victim of a conspiracy?'

'I can't say that I do.' Honeybath's surprise increased. He even felt a certain discomfort in face of the sharply appraising glance with which Michaelis had accompanied these questions. 'And may we turn,' he asked firmly, 'to one or two more specific issues? It's very probable, Dr Michaelis, that it would be my intention to go on painting.'

'Ah! Yes, indeed.' Michaelis was at once enthusiastic. 'Titian is the great exemplar there. Went on painting far into his nineties. Splendid fellow!'

'Titian mayn't even have lived into his nineties.' Honeybath was conscious of rather snapping this out—perhaps at being displeased at hearing a celebrated painter patronized in this way. 'And my point is a simple one, Dr Michaelis. I'd have to be assured of a room with a good north light.'

'But of course!' The Medical Superintendent betrayed surprise that there should be any question about this. 'At Hanwell we regard such matters as of the utmost importance. Everything must be done to sustain our residents in their sense of useful occupation.'

'As with Lady Munden and her seaweed.'

'Exactly so. How pleasant that you know Lady Munden.'

'And Colonel Dacre and his rifle-range.' Honeybath was about to add 'And the man with the electronic golf-ball.' But he reflected that here he had perhaps been made the recipient of a confidential disclosure, which he ought not to pass on. 'I quite agree about the importance of having something to do in one's old age,' he said. 'Knitting or chess or abstruse mathematical calculation: it all comes to the same thing, no doubt. With me it will be painting, as long as my eyesight holds.'

'And, what is more important, your inspiration.' Michaelis produced this comparative estimate with confidence. 'I feel nothing is of more importance here than the creating of favourable conditions for the exercise of the artistic temperament.'

Honeybath was rather at a loss before this. He supposed the chap meant well—but here, surely, was a whiff of sales-talk after all.

'Don't you feel it to be rather tricky ground?' he asked. 'It's often under unfavourable conditions that what you call the artistic temperament seems to make out best.'

'A most interesting paradox.' Michaelis nodded gravely, with the air of an intelligent man properly open to instruction by an expert. 'And I agree, of course, that inspiration is a most unpredictable thing. You hear its voice, and have to obey.'

'Inspiration isn't a voice. It's a breath.' Honeybath made the pedantic point a shade crossly, having grown rather tired of this conversation.

'Ah, yes. But surely, Mr Honeybath, you hear voices from time to time—advising you to do a thing one way and avoid another? It's a common trait among artists, I believe.'

'I don't think you believe anything of the sort. And the assertion is nonsense, in any case.' Honeybath was suddenly very angry. 'Dr Michaelis, please don't take me for a fool. It may be your duty to assess intending residents here in terms of their nervous stability, or liability to neurosis, or whatever the jargon is. But spare me this fishing around for notions of persecution and auditory hallucinations. And I shall withdraw my application here, since I have clearly been misinformed. I had no idea that it has the character of a clinic for the mentally deranged.' Honeybath rose to his feet. 'And I regret that the misapprehension has resulted in my wasting your time.'

'But it's nothing of the sort!' Dr Michaelis had sprung to his feet too, and appeared extremely upset. 'And I do apologize Mr Honeybath, for having been so clumsy. It is perfectly true that I am obliged a little to sound the nervous constitution of our applicants. But the reason is this : we have to be careful to accept as residents here only a small number—you may call it a quota—of persons in any way eccentrically disposed. To take that small number, we regard as a social duty. And I assure you that, so far, our policy has been a complete success. Our lives are so arranged here that nobody's privacy need be invaded by anybody else, and such oddities as a few of our guests exhibit do no more than—how shall I express it?—make for interest. And the people who *are* a trifle strange benefit enormously from remaining in normal society under conditions so carefully controlled that it is impossible for them to be the slightest nuisance to anybody. That, quite simply, is the state of our case, Mr Honeybath. I hope, therefore, that you will reconsider the matter in the light of my remarks.'

Charles Honeybath ought, perhaps, to have said 'Damn your remarks, sir!' and departed from Hanwell Court without more ado. This would have been uncivil—even unpardonable in view of the fact that Michaelis had gone to some trouble to explain the set-up within which he clearly made a perfectly honourable living. But at least it would have got the situation straight, since Honeybath for some reason now knew in his heart that he would never become an inmate of this curious establishment. But he was sensitive about his position. He had gone some little way in committing himself to the place, and now he had the

appearance of shying away from it because it had been
revealed to him that, on the most respectable grounds of
social conscience and policy, it afforded shelter and support
to a small proportion of harmless cranks. True, they were
affluent cranks, and somebody made a profit out of them
somewhere. But the arrangement was laudable rather than
censurable in any way, and if he now bolted because it had
been revealed to him he would in fact be doing injustice to
his own tolerably liberal mind. His turning away from
Hanwell Court as Honeybath's haven was really prompted
(a little introspection told him) by something quite different
and not easily analysed or expressed. The place just wasn't
him. It had been revealed to him—to put it bluntly—that
he'd rather end his days in a garret than at Hanwell's
opulent remove from the common traffic of life. But he
couldn't decently decant this feeling on young Dr Michaelis,
and he decided (weakly, perhaps) that he must ease himself
out of a false situation by temporizing means.

'I'm grateful to you for explaining things,' he therefore
said. 'And I'll come to no final decision in a hurry.'

'That is everything we could hope for, Mr Honeybath.'
Dr Michaelis was now composed—even smooth—again.
'And, meanwhile, I wonder whether we might now go and
hunt for that room with a good northern light? Even if you
don't want it yourself, you might have a fellow-artist to
whom you would wish to recommend it. And I'd like you to
be assured of the sincerity with which I speak when I say
how much I'd like to see Hanwell being useful to a few
distinguished artists, or writers, or the like, in their later
years. Not that the distinction is all that important. It's the
lifetime's dedication to the hard labour of art that counts
with me.'

Honeybath listened, and again felt himself to have rather
a liking for Michaelis. The man had made an honest and

not ignoble little speech. So he allowed himself to be guided through the splendid building once more, and presently the appropriate quarters were found : a great high room with perfect lighting, and with attached to it a small and secluded sitting-room having a glorious view over the park and a distant line of downs—this and a bedroom and bathroom all firmly behind the occupant's own front door. A more nearly perfect disposition of things for a solitary artist of advancing years it would have been hard to conceive. It failed to shake Honeybath, but at least it enabled him to be abundant in civil expressions. He ended by lunching in Hanwell Court along with those of the inmates opting for public refection at this time of day. People sat at their own small tables at a well-calculated remove each from the other. You could converse with a neighbour without shouting, or without unsociability you could treat yourself as being in solitude. The fare was excellent, and there was the unobtrusive adjuvant of a capital hock.

After this, Honeybath sought out Michaelis again, took a politely non-committal farewell, and got away. The notion that he might commend the place to somebody else didn't again enter his head. But it was to do so fatefully—indeed, fatally—in the not distant future.

VII

EDWIN LIGHTFOOT WAS back in England. He had
been back in England—and in Royal Crescent, Holland
Park—for some weeks before Honeybath heard of it. The
news came to him, once more, through the agency of
Lightfoot's brother-in-law, Ambrose Prout. And Prout, as
on a previous occasion, was extremely worried. He entered
Honeybath's studio one morning—he virtually broke in—
with the plain object of spreading despondency and alarm.
At first Honeybath simply resented the irruption. He had
no sitter with him, it was true, but he was engaged on the
tricky if not wholly unfamiliar task of transferring to a
canvas the Robes and Star of the Order of the Garter as
these august habiliments were disposed in front of him,
draped upon a kind of tailor's dummy adapted for the
purpose. The Star was proving particularly awkward; he
had set it at an oblique angle to the picture-plane, and it
was refusing to look like the resplendent gewgaw it was.

'Melissa's attitude worries me,' Prout said. 'I feel she
isn't behaving well. She ought to go back to him—and see
that he gets on with his work.'

'What has happened to the flat?'

'The lease has gone to a car-salesman, I believe.'

'Well, Ambrose, one can't expect Melissa to live in that
attic studio. She'd feel it to be a come-down.'

'Or a go-up.' Prout seemed not to find his own witticism
encouraging. 'And the point is that Edwin can't live there

either. Not what could be called living. It's chaotic. He hasn't a clue.'

'I rather feared it might be like that.' Honeybath had abandoned his palette. 'What about that Mrs Plover? I had a notion she might rally round once Melissa had departed. It's only about Melissa she makes really dark remarks.'

'And I don't blame her.' Prout offered this unbrotherly sentiment gloomily. 'I got on to Mrs Plover, and she went in once or twice. But the other woman offended her.'

'The other woman?' There was astonishment in Honeybath's voice. 'You don't mean to say that Edwin has set up with a mistress?'

'Not exactly that. An occasional professional visitor, you might say. But it seems she and Mrs Plover happened to collide. Twice, I believe. And, to quote Mrs Plover, words passed.'

'It's not seemly—not at Edwin's age.' Honeybath was genuinely dismayed by this fresh evidence of disorderly living on the part of his old friend.

'He can afford it. Edwin could afford a seraglio, if he had a mind to it.'

'Well, that's something. It had occurred to me to wonder whether he and Melissa were a bit hard up. Investments gone to pot, or something like that.'

'Not a bit of it. It's having money that has always been Edwin's trouble, not lacking it. I've told you that before, Charles. It seduced him from honest labour when he was at the top of his form. And now, if he *did* lose his private income, it wouldn't be possible to sell his pictures to seaside hotels.' This dire verdict came from Prout with dark conviction. 'As for that studio, the public health people are likely to be on about it at any time. It stinks.'

'Good heavens!'

'Half-empty cans of beer and half-empty bottles of milk.

And the remains of kippers and potted shrimps.' Prout shook his head. 'Unbelievable, isn't it? There was always something of the epicure about Edwin. He must suffer atrociously. And he could afford to dine where he chose every night of the week! Do you think he can have gone agoraphobic?'

'No, I don't. I'd suppose him simply to be dispirited and out of sorts.' Honeybath judged it sensible to discount extravagant interpretations of his friend's disarray. 'Perhaps being alone in Italy wasn't a success. When he *is* alone, by the way, do you think he goes in for that freakish nonsense of being somebody else? It was a burglar, you remember, at the time of his bust-up with Melissa.'

'Edwin has gone up in the world since then. The last time I saw him, he had draped himself in a sheet and was declaring he was Praxiteles. Or it may have been Zeuxis. I forget.'

'Zeuxis seems the more probable.' Honeybath divested himself of the smock which he affected when painting. 'At least it isn't madness, his putting on those turns. It amused him when he was a student.'

'That he once did it when sane doesn't mean that he doesn't now do it when dotty.' Prout seemed determined to take the darkest view of his brother-in-law's condition. 'I just don't know what we can do.'

'We can go and see him now,' Honeybath said. 'Both of us. I'll call a cab.'

This brisk resolution, had Prout known it, was the product of an unflattering estimate of his reliability as a witness which Honeybath had formed of him long ago. Indeed, Honeybath didn't really care for Prout any more than he did for his irritating sister. Prout, so far as he knew, was tolerably honest in his business dealings, but he tended to see both persons and situations reflected in the somewhat distorting mirror of his own self-interest. He might well be representing Lightfoot's condition as more hopeless than it was merely because the painter was no longer among his more profitable clients. Didn't he always come back to Edwin's idleness, or presumed idleness, as a point of grievance? Viewing Prout as he thus did, it was perhaps curious that Honeybath should have so promptly insisted on having his company on this visit to Lightfoot now. But it seemed to Honeybath that, all things considered, a reconciliation between Edwin and Melissa was the best thing to go for. It was likely, at least, to put a stop to the indignity of Edwin's fatuously entangling himself with low women. (This had shocked Honeybath very much—offending a strain of puritanical feeling in him such as artists are not popularly supposed much to indulge.) And if he was to develop some plan for bringing Edwin and Melissa together, it would be sensible to involve Melissa's brother from the start. This was why he was now bundling Prout into a taxi.

'Not that he *can* have done all that little,' Prout said, as soon as they moved off. 'I've never quite believed it. It doesn't make sense.'

'Ambrose, just what are you talking about?'

'Edwin's golden decade, of course. I read some elderly critic calling it that the other day. Mind you, it was nearer five years than ten. There's a word for a five-year period.'

'A quinquennium. Or a lustre.'

'That's it—a lustre. And when a chap is at the peak of his performance like that, it's almost certain he'll work like mad. That's what I mean by saying that the scarcity of early Lightfoots doesn't make sense. There *must* be more of them. Somehow or other, they've gone underground.'

'Mere speculation, Ambrose.' Honeybath spoke rather shortly, having heard this jeremiad before. It was almost an obsession of Prout's. 'I was fairly intimate with Edwin in those days, and it's my impression that he found achieving that handful of masterpieces totally exhausting. Even if he'd been right down on the bread-line he couldn't have done more of them. There may be one or two in somebody's cold storage. It's impossible to tell. But I just don't believe in the theory of a whole cache of them. I've told you so before.'

'Only a month ago I thought I'd run one to earth.' Prout had paid no attention to these remarks. 'An old woman called Gutermann-Seuss. You know the name?'

'There was an expatriate German *Kunsthändler* called that, I remember. He lived in Brighton.'

'Well, this was his widow—and living in Brighton. I had it on a most reliable grape-vine that she possessed one of the things. And that she was uncommonly hard up.'

'It sounded promising, no doubt.'

'Certainly it did—particularly as she was reported as not particularly knowledgeable in her late husband's line of business.'

'So that there was a good chance of driving an outrageous bargain with the old soul?' Prout wasn't to be blamed, Honeybath supposed, for subscribing to ethical standards which had doubtless been the late Mr Gutermann-Seuss's as well. But this talk was distasteful, all the same. 'But it was a mare's nest?'

'Absolutely. What she possessed proved to be a worthless affair on which some crook had forged Edwin's signature. Disgraceful, wouldn't you say? It had sent me on a fool's errand.'

'Too bad, Ambrose.' Honeybath, although inclined to share Prout's indignation from a somewhat different point of view, managed to be amused. 'I hope you didn't tell Edwin. It might have upset him.'

'Of course I didn't. The whole subject of the lustre, or whatever it's to be called, is tabu with him. He's a most unreasonable man, even in his moments of sanity.'

'Too bad that your sister married him. And we have to try to get some reasonableness into him now. But we shan't do it by badgering him. So we'll go easy with Edwin, Ambrose. Just see if you can manage a quietly sympathetic response to anything he has to say.' Having delivered this admonition—or rebuke—Honeybath remained silent for the remainder of the journey to Holland Park. It hadn't after all been a good idea, he told himself, to bring Ambrose Prout along. But he could hardly turn the fellow out of the taxi now.

They reached the former abode of the Lightfoots, and Honeybath paid the fare. They entered, and passed a prosperous-looking man coming down the stairs. It was probably the car-salesman, Honeybath thought. The lizard rather than the lion. They climbed to the studio, on the door of which Prout gave an ominously impatient knock. There was no bell. And there was no answer either. Prout pushed open the door, and they went in. The place did smell. This phenomenon seemed to deliver a clear message to Honeybath. Sympathy, yes. But action as well.

The first objects Honeybath's eye fell upon were a canvas on the easel and a palette perched on a high stool near by. Edwin had been at work. Honeybath took a second look at the canvas, and felt something like a stab of pain. No good painter had produced anything so pitiful as this since the final degeneration of Utrillo. And Edwin had never been a drunkard, let alone a drug addict. Something had recently gone very far wrong.

What had gone wrong was Edwin himself, whether in mind or body. Edwin was sitting in a corner of the studio. He was sitting on the floor. It was an unnecessary posture, since the bleak place did run to two or three reasonably serviceable-looking chairs. Edwin sat on the floor, and looked from Honeybath to Prout and from Prout to Honeybath.

But he didn't speak. He wasn't able to speak, since he was fully occupied in soundlessly weeping.

'Good God, the man's mad!' Prout cried out. 'I knew it would happen, and here it is. Clean out of his mind.'

'Ambrose, don't be a fool.' Prout, Honeybath saw, was as terrified as if he had never seen emotional distress before. But this by no means excused the indecency of his reaction. 'Put a kettle on that gas ring, and see if you can make some tea. Edwin, my dear man, get up and come and sit here by the window. There are things to talk about. You're not at all well, and we must get you right again.'

'I can't do anything. I can't do anything at all!' The dejected Lightfoot had got to his feet unsteadily. He pointed towards the easel. 'Look at it,' he said.

'It's what I've just done, and we can both give it a rest.' As he said this Honeybath lifted the canvas from the easel, carried it to the far end of the studio, and dumped it without ceremony behind a tattered Japanese screen. His return route took him past the big table on which Lightfoot kept his drawing-board and a litter of pencils, charcoal and chalks. Lying on it were a couple of the strongly accented portrait-sketches of men that Honeybath had noticed on his last visit. These were again wet-paper affairs. And the paper *was* wet. The sketches were quite new—and were masterly in their kind.

'You've got yourself wrong, Edwin,' Honeybath said. He spoke as if to one entirely composed, although in fact Lightfoot could have been described as still blubbering. 'You think you've lost everything, and in fact you're only a bit browned off on oils. Inside every *malerisch* artist, you know, there's a linear one screaming to be let out. And you're giving yours a chance in those portrait heads. They're tiptop.'

'There's no tea,' Prout said.

'Then go out and buy some, Ambrose. And a bottle of

milk and a packet of cigarettes. Bestir yourself, man.' Honeybath spoke with brisk command. If he didn't clear up this
mess, nobody else would.

'Not true. Everything gone. I can't even draw.' These
assertions came from Lightfoot punctuated by distressing
snivels. It was useless to blink the fact that he was in a most
abject state.

'Come over here, Edwin.' Honeybath had remained beside
the table, on which he was now securing with drawing-pins
a large sheet of cartridge-paper. 'Giotto's circle,' he said, as
Lightfoot shambled up. 'You remember, Edwin? I could
beat you sometimes, but not often. Here goes.' He picked
up a crayon, and with a single sweep of his wrist (the un-
injured wrist) contrived a very tolerable approximation to a
circle some ten inches in diameter. 'Next boy,' he said.

Lightfoot produced one large sniff, took the crayon, and
obediently drew his circle. It was a perfect circle. A pair of
compasses couldn't have faulted it.

'You win,' Honeybath said. 'So you can draw, can't you?'

'So I can.' Lightfoot sounded surprised but entirely convinced. He appeared so satisfied for the moment, indeed,
that Honeybath was taken aback. The little demonstration
just concluded hadn't really all that to do with 'drawing' as
an artist understands the term. But he remembered that
Edwin had always been a curiously suggestible type. He
would believe what he was confidently told about himself,
although the belief didn't always stick. Even when he was
kidding himself he was Flannel Foot or Zeuxis something of
the same disposition must be at work. Honeybath was not
sanguine enough to suppose that 'his primitive stroke of
therapy had effected much. But at least Edwin now sat
down, and didn't again fall to weeping. And when Prout
returned with a bottle of milk and a packet of tea he

watched the production of a beverage from these simple
constituents with a kind of quiescent puzzled respect.

Honeybath had to wash some cups. There was no denying
that the studio was in a most disgusting mess. Edwin had
obviously persuaded himself—or been injudiciously persuaded by others—that he couldn't do a damn thing in a
domestic way, and not a damn thing was he going to do.
But it was clear that the chaos around him gave him no
emotional satisfaction even of the most perverse sort. He was
perfectly miserable before the spectacle of the squalor he had
himself created. So here was an absolute datum—and one
Honeybath had really acknowledged already. There was no
future for Edwin in this confounded place.

Prout didn't contribute to any achieving of an atmosphere
of repose. Having made the tea, he was prowling restlessly
here and there, stirring up the dust and making disgusted
noises when he trammelled his fingers in cobweb. He even
opened the deep cupboards that ran under the eaves and
peered inside, possibly in his obsessive pursuit of vanished
Lightfoot masterpieces. This behaviour presently unsettled
Lightfoot in a new way. He got to his feet again and began
himself to wander round. It wasn't aimlessly, although he
was in fact making efforts that it should appear so. Honeybath, puzzled at first, became aware that there were half a
dozen objects in the studio—a door-knob, a mackintosh
hanging on a peg, an empty biscuit tin and the like—which
Edwin was under some constraint to touch in a set order.
He was trying now to achieve this without detection, and
the furtive effect thus produced was at once pathetic and
embarrassing. Edwin might have been a pickpocket, edging
his way warily towards a prospect. Honeybath would rather
have had him wholeheartedly a burglar again. But it was
clear that Flannel Foot had vanished below Edwin's imaginative horizon, probably for keeps.

These two compulsive individuals together were a bit much. Honeybath saw that it would take more than jokes about Giotto's circle to haul Edwin back into a normal frame of mind, and that the next step must be to call in medical assistance. He was wondering how best to set about this when the door opened without ceremony and Mrs Plover came into the studio. Although Mrs Plover was not one professionally qualified to deal with mental disturbance she was at least not mentally disturbed herself. Honeybath inclined, therefore, to welcome her as an ally to whom a cordial greeting was due. But for the moment Mrs Plover ignored him, being more interested in Ambrose Prout. Prout, somewhat unfortunately, was down on his hands and knees peering into the depths of a cupboard; he no doubt imagined himself to have descried something promising hidden away in it.

'Oho!' Mrs Plover said. She had placed her arms akimbo, like some stage version of herself in low comedy. 'Nosey Parker, is it? I seen 'im at it afore, I 'ave.' Mrs Plover was addressing Prout, much as if under the influence of Melissa's third-person-singular approach to conversation. 'Looking for what 'e can lay 'is 'ands on, is he?' She now did turn to Honeybath. 'And taking adwantages on the poor afflicted gentleman for his own narsty ends, whatsomever they may be. Mr Ell 'e'd be better orf wiv 'is trollop, I'd say. Not that in 'is present state Mr Ell's fit to go to bed with the cat. But at least the poor girl is arfter no more than a five-pound note. You ought to be calling in the law, Mr Haich, and that's the short and the long of it.'

Prout, thus aspersed as one detected in petty larceny, addressed his accuser loudly as a silly bitch. Honeybath, finding his grave anxieties thus suddenly implicated with an episode of unseemly farce, did for a moment actually think of the police, although domestic *fracas* like the present were

distinctly not of an order with which policemen care to
deal. Nor, indeed, could he reasonably call an ambulance,
unless Mrs Plover did something like picking up a chair
and hitting Prout over the head. Edwin, it was true, had
taken to soundlessly weeping again, as a man whom the
world has finally overcome. But what that seemed to call
for was a family doctor with a hypodermic or a swiftly-
acting pill. He had no idea whether the Lightfoots ran to
anybody of the sort. So he had, for the moment, only his
own authority to rely on. He bundled Mrs Plover (who had
certainly turned up with the best intentions) out of the
studio. He wrote the name and telephone number of his
own doctor on a card, and instructed Prout to go and call
him up at once, explaining himself as a relation of the
afflicted man. Then he settled down (if it could be called
that) to keep an eye on Edwin. For the thought had come
to him that poor Edwin had arrived at a point at which he
might do himself some mischief.

And this proved to be a professional opinion too. By that
evening the distressed painter had withdrawn into a nursing
home and was secure for a time. Honeybath was enormously relieved, and even found satisfaction in the circumstance that a nervous breakdown is a perfectly respectable
misfortune with nothing unseemly about it. But a long-term
problem remained. It was solved, or appeared to be solved,
when Edwin was persuaded, after his convalescence, to take
up Honeybath's place at Hanwell Court.

PART TWO

MYSTERY AT HANWELL COURT

VIII

SOME TWO YEARS after the foregoing section of our
narrative concludes, Lady Munden (leaving her seaweed to
sink or swim) went to London to spend a few days in the
comfortable dwelling of an old school-friend, Lady Celia
Clandon. Lady Munden, although a woman of strong
character, was no more than the widow of a prosperous
manufacturer, whereas Lady Celia was the spinster daughter
of a person in an altogether more exalted rank of society.
There was here a good English reason for Lady Munden's
being distinctly under Lady Celia's thumb; and there was
another—equally English and equally valid—in the circumstance that Lady Celia had been Captain of Lacrosse when
the future Lady Munden held only a very uncertain place
in the First Twelve.

But Lady Celia, although thus athletically distinguished,
also took a keen interest (as became a member of the
aristocracy) in Culture at large and in the Arts in particular.
This being so, and the month being June, she naturally
took her guest to the Annual Exhibition promoted by the
Royal Academy in a building admirably sited for those
visitors who, after adequate aesthetic delectation, like to re-
cruit themselves by taking luncheon at Claridge's or the Ritz.
Still a vigorous pedestrian, Lady Celia never flinched from
doing the whole show, and she paraded Lady Munden
through the galleries both great and small, not even omitting
those minor ones that accommodate drawings, water-colour

77

sketches, lithographs, and architectural performances which may or may not one day make the bold advance out of two dimensions into three. It was in these circumstances that Lady Munden, already in a condition of some fatigue, was suddenly confronted with herself in a pencil sketch facetiously entitled *Kelp, Sweet Kelp: Who buys my Pretty Kelp?* There she was, habited as a kind of flower-girl from a print such as might illustrate *The Cries of Old London*, and holding up in an enticing manner a large strand of the stuff known to the learned as belonging to the *Laminariaceae.*

Lady Munden was not amused. She was, in fact, outraged —and the more so because the reaction of her august friend took the form of far too audible mirth. As Lady Celia's laughter rang out (and laughter *does* ring out if scandalously released in Burlington House) Lady Munden consulted her catalogue and discovered that the perpetrator of the outrage was one Edwin Lightfoot R.A. The name struck some sort of chord, and the letters after it told her that the impertinence had not been perpetrated by some stripling, some mere tadpole of the arts. Without pausing to consult her recollection further, however, she marched off to what she took to be the appropriate desk and demanded satisfaction at once. All she learnt was that she might buy the thing for a hundred guineas, and take possession of her property at the close of the Exhibition. Lady Celia then took her downstairs to the bar, and obliged her to consume a large gin and vermouth. Under the inspiration of this she was able to recall that the atrocious Lightfoot was an eccentric little man who had been most injudiciously admitted into residence at Hanwell Court a couple of years before.

Lady Munden had thoughts of her solicitor, who was to be found in Lincoln's Inn. But her solicitor was an unsatisfactory creature, grossly complacent before the machinations of her despicable trustees, and she decided that

Brigadier Luxmoore was the more promising person to tackle. The Brigadier was at least a gentleman : it was the most obtrusive of his qualifications for holding down the job of running Hanwell Court. On the following morning Lady Munden cut short her sampling of the pleasures of the town and returned to her country retreat.

Brigadier Luxmore was all sympathy. He was also all for discretion. Mr Lightfoot, he explained, was a man of somewhat unstable temperament—she must have observed this —and Dr Michaelis judged it important that he should be encouraged to potter at activities which, it appeared, he had once pursued with quite reasonable success. Artists must be permitted a certain indulgence, must they not ? But in future an eye would be kept, of course, on this particular creative urge on his part. In the meantime, and since it would clearly be disagreeable to Lady Munden to have any further concern in the matter, he, the Brigadier, would himself undertake to purchase the offensive object and destroy it out of hand as soon as it came into his possession. And no expense to Lady Munden herself would be involved. He was quite certain that his directors would approve any disbursement he would have to make.

A hundred guineas is a hundred guineas. Lady Munden was considerably mollified. She even undertook not to spread the scandalous story around. By this (although she didn't say so) she didn't mean that she would withhold the disgraceful episode from her more intimate friends. And in fact she told it to Colonel Dacre and the Misses Pinchon at bridge that evening. So by the following day this highly confidential intelligence was known (in every sort of distorted form) to almost everybody at Hanwell Court.

And at least in one direction it spread beyond that. Melissa Lightfoot, having tired of the parrot, had taken up something called Deep Meditation instead—practising it alike among a small group of enlightened persons and in the solitude of a comfortable service flat to which she had withdrawn just off Victoria Street. The discipline to which she was subjecting herself, however, didn't insulate her from the world and its diurnal concerns so exclusively as to prevent her keeping tabs on her husband. Why she found this necessary wasn't clear, and indeed conflicted with the frequent vehement assurances she offered her friends that seeing the back of Edwin had acted as a kind of Release into the Infinite. Be this as it may, Melissa maintained a regular correspondence with one of the Misses Pinchon (residents in Hanwell Court so dim that absolutely nothing need be chronicled about them). It was thus that she heard of her husband's prank at the expense of Lady Munden, and she immediately passed on the news to her brother. It was still Ambrose Prout's conviction that his brother-in-law was entirely mad. The sad truth of the matter (he would confide to his intimates) was that probably no artistic genius had gone madder since Nijinsky. But this didn't prevent Prout from taking a laudable interest in Edwin's life in retirement. Was he by any chance drawing or painting in the intervals of climbing up the curtains and chewing the carpet? It was perhaps in Prout's mind that there was at least a modest market for visionary performances by deranged professional artists. And even by amateurs, provided they were sufficiently famous in some other way. Here Nijinsky turned up again. When no longer able to dance a step he had produced weird pictures any example of which produced a good price nowadays.

Possibly with these thoughts in mind, Prout made yet another of his descents upon Charles Honeybath. They must both go down to Hanwell at once. Edwin's indiscretion might well have got him into ill-favour there, in which case immediate steps ought to be taken to smooth things out.

Honeybath, although distressed by the news, wasn't too keen on a joint expedition. On the occasion of the crisis in Royal Crescent Prout's comportment towards his brother-in-law had been distinctly censurable. And Edwin, he knew, no longer suffered Prout's society at all gladly; this had become clear from Edwin's conversation on several of the frequent occasions upon which Honeybath had run down to visit his old friend himself. It seemed probable that his company was being sought on this expedition merely to assist Prout in gaining admission to the presence of his alienated relative. But despite this suspicion, Honeybath acquiesced in the proposal. It interested him to know that Edwin was continuing to produce those strange sketches. As likenesses, at least, they must still be tiptop if the absurd Lady Munden had instantly recognized herself as the Seaweed Girl of Burlington House. Edwin still had some vitality as an artist. At the back of Honeybath's mind there even lay the thought that it might be up to him to get Edwin away from Hanwell and restored to the society of his peers. He had misgivings about his own wisdom in having been the instrument of dumping Edwin in that dubious haven in the first place.

When they arrived at Hanwell Court, however, the visit didn't work out in the manner proposed. Somewhat unexpectedly, and when they were moving smoothly up the drive in the establishment's Rolls, Prout suggested a change of plan. It might upset Edwin, he said, if the two of them presented themselves simultaneously. It might put him in mind of that last painful occasion upon which the three of them had been closeted together. So he would go first, and Honeybath would follow a little later. And if Edwin proved 'awkward' Prout would get hold of the fellow Michaelis to restore order.

Honeybath decided not to object to this new arrangement,

which he put down to a kind of jealousy or possessiveness in regard to Edwin which surfaced in Prout from time to time. Moreover he resented Prout's obstinate insistence, constantly evident in his chosen terminology, that Edwin was definitely off his head. Honeybath's own impression here was that (just as in the Flannel Foot business) it amused Edwin to play mad Hamlet. But there were those who took the view that it is precisely in pretending to be mad that the Prince of Denmark's true madness consists. This is a confused idea. But then the spectacle of random and inter- mittent scattiness is confusing.

On the more recent of his previous visits to Hanwell Court Honeybath had concluded that Edwin was in many ways well suited by the place. He undoubtedly appreciated its material comforts. He could be quite funny about the other inmates (he had taken over 'inmates' from his friend) in a way that showed at least an occasional sharp awareness of them. This was much to the good—for hadn't solitude become one of Edwin's principal enemies? On the other hand he could still be very restless—to a degree, indeed, which Honeybath had gathered it required the arts of Dr Michaelis to cope with. Moreover, and this was something rather new, Edwin had become curiously secretive and wary. It was almost as if he had something to hide, and as if that something in itself obscurely puzzled him. Honeybath found all this difficult to assess, and it was perhaps behind his lurking feeling that, despite the fairly even tenor of things at Hanwell hitherto, it was perhaps his duty to get Edwin away. All in all, he was conscious of a need to bring his thoughts together before this fresh encounter. So it was quite contentedly that, just as on a previous occasion, he now went off on a short procrastinating stroll through the gardens. He even decided, this time, to go a little farther afield and explore the park as well.

IX

IT WAS BECAUSE the idea of exploration was in his head that Honeybath decided to begin by having another go at that maze. He still remembered his former behaviour in it as slightly ludicrous. He remembered, too, assuring the gardener who had then surprised him that he might penetrate to some sort of aviary at the centre of the thing upon a later occasion. Parakeets had been mentioned. He'd go and take a look at the birds.

It wasn't in the least difficult. The birds helped. On his previous visit they must have been asleep; now they screeched and squawked in a manner that provided bearings of a sort. But the noise wasn't otherwise attractive, so that Honeybath thought he'd have done better to make straight for the park, above which larks were singing in an appropriate way. But now here he was at the centre of the labyrinth. He glimpsed the parakeets and then ceased to notice them. For the place had another visitor. It was the man in the Panama hat.

'Good morning,' Honeybath said—being determined to be, as it were, quick on the draw this time. But the Panama man displayed an identical determination, and more rapidly still. In his case, moreover, there was nothing merely metaphorical about it. His right hand had disappeared under his left armpit in a manner that Honeybath (who had a weakness for gangster films) could interpret in only one way. But this untoward behaviour instantly cancelled itself,

and what the Panama man actually produced was an innocuous silk handkerchief. With this he dabbed in a ritual
manner at his brow.

'Warm day,' he said. 'How do you do? My name is
Brown.' He was keeping a careful eye on Honeybath's
hands. 'Brown,' he repeated a little more loudly—much as
if prompted to refute a false persuasion on Honeybath's part
that his name was in fact Green or Gray. 'Seen you here
before, I think?' Mr Brown said. 'Just calling in? No more
than that?'

'Precisely so. My name is Honeybath, and I am merely
visiting a friend.' Honeybath glanced at the aviary, which
at least suggested a conversational resource. 'Are you
fond of birds?' he asked.

'Never see one now.' Mr Brown spoke with sudden gloom.
'Or not under sixty or thereabout.'

'Ah, is that so?' For a moment Honeybath was a little at
sea, and he even reflected that members of the parrot family
are notably long-lived. When the force of Mr Brown's col-
loquialism came home to him, however, he recalled the
gardener's informing him that the man with the Panama
hat was one of the shy ones. Presumably Brown had been
explaining that this disability lay particularly heavily upon
him in regard to young female persons. But since this
appeared not a suitable subject for discussion with an
acquaintance of only a couple of minutes' standing Honeybath became more explicit. 'You must have got to know
those parakeets quite well,' he said. 'If, as I imagine, this
is a favourite haunt of yours.'

'Quite right,' Mr Brown said emphatically. 'Peaceful
creatures, aren't they? Birds of a feather, you might say.
And yet never so much as a peck or a scratch between
them.'

'Is that so?' It might have been said that Honeybath

hadn't quite followed that argument here. 'They look well
cared for and comfortable,' he offered vaguely.

'Just that.' Mr Brown was emphatic once more. 'Just
like they'd been nicked, in a manner of speaking. Not that
all them that are inside are that. Comfortable, perhaps—
although the food is cruelly uninteresting at times. But no
security that would set a man's mind at rest. Believe you
me, anything can happen at any time, once a man's inside.
You needn't even have grassed—or nothing to speak of.'

'Most interesting.' Honeybath, a man of acute perception,
realized that Mr Brown must be commenting on conditions
obtaining in Her Majesty's prisons. It was again a peculiar
topic of conversation, and the more so because of a certain
air with which Mr Brown delivered himself of it. He spoke
with entire ease, and as one perfectly conversant with the
canons observed in what might be called upper-class chit-
chat. But there was undeniably something socially anomalous
in Mr Brown. Was he one who had risen from below the
middle station of life to sudden affluence, perhaps by win-
ning an enormous 'dividend' on the pools? Had he done
this, opted for the genteel idleness of Hanwell Court, and
taken some random and uncertain steps (such as buying a
supply of Panama hats) in living up to his new station? But
if this was so, why was he drawn to topics unlikely to be of
much concern to the law-abiding sections of society? And
why was his idiom almost obtrusively that of the imperfectly educated? He undoubtedly counted as an inmate,
since Honeybath had once or twice glimpsed him in the
interior of the house when making previous visits to Lightfoot. Was it possible—this really brilliant idea came to
Honeybath like a flash—that Brown was another sufferer
from Flannel Foot disease, a perfectly respectable citizen
gaining some perverse satisfaction from hinting a background
in low life and criminal practice? Was it even conceivable

that Edwin had put him up to it, had passed on the Flannel
Foot game to a new player? This was an extravagant notion,
and Honeybath dismissed it. But he did wonder whether
this new acquaintance would have anything to say about
Edwin. Had he been aware, for instance, of the storm in a
teacup over Lady Munden?

'I suppose,' he asked, 'you know my friend Lightfoot,
whom I've come to visit? He has been here for a couple of
years now. And so, I believe, have you.'

'Oh, yes—I know *him*.' Brown had produced a swiftly
wary glance—rather in Edwin's manner, Honeybath reflected, but considerably more intense. 'One of the nutters,
some of them take him for. But you can never tell, you
know. I've read a story somewhere of a man who faked it
he was loco, just to seem harmless and innocent-like when
he had it in for another guy.'

'I believe it to be an archetypal theme.' Seeing that this
learned comment made little impression on Mr Brown,
Honeybath added, 'But you wouldn't think of my friend
Lightfoot as being like that? He couldn't entertain malign
designs against you.'

'You can't ever be sure, if you ask me. Not of anybody.'

This was a distressing remark. It suggested—as seemed
only too probable—that mildly paranoid feelings blew rather
freely around Hanwell Court.

'Oh, come, Mr Brown!' Honeybath essayed a robust
note. 'You've known me for about ten minutes. But you'd
trust me with your wallet, wouldn't you, with no misgiving
at all? One knows at once these simple things about a
man.'

'I don't say you're wrong there, Mr Honeybath. Not in
certain cases that is. Sometimes I can take a good look at a
man—keeping my distance, mark you, and my head low—
and I can see he's on the square.'

'Perhaps you'll put me in that category sufficiently to join me in my short walk?' Honeybath asked this on an odd impulse; it was as if he felt that with Brown he was on the tip of the tail of something he wanted to get hold of. It was a wholly irrational feeling. 'Just up to that statue, perhaps, at the head of the drive.'

'I'll be very happy, I'm sure.' Brown said this with a considerable air of magnanimity. 'And one gets out of this maze in no time, you know. It's easier to get out than to get in. Which isn't the case with you know where.'

As this could only be a further reference to incarceration under penal conditions, Honeybath was constrained to conclude that Mr Brown was the victim of something like an *idée fixe*. The condition, he believed, could be an extremely painful one—almost as bad as an agonizing phobia. Brown didn't, indeed, have the air of a man positively haunted, but this was perhaps due to the ministrations of Dr Michaelis—whose main function, Honeybath had by now come to understand, was to assist those of the inmates who had come to Hanwell under the quota system. Yet this explanation didn't quite account for Brown, and particularly for his perplexingly plebeian facet. And now Honeybath had another brilliant idea. (He was surprisingly prolific in these.) Brown belonged to that rapidly increasing number of persons who have been highly successful financiers in their time but who, having been a shade neglectful of certain niceties of the law, have been obliged to spend a considerable term of years (as Brown would express it) 'inside'. Much in the manners, and even mode of speech, of those with whom they had thus for long associated would almost unavoidably rub off on them. Brown, in fact, was what was vulgarly termed an old lag. Before being 'nicked' he had providently salted away a competence adequate to maintain him in his present honourable retirement.

'This way out,' Brown was saying. 'The middle of the maze isn't at the middle at all—twig? It's right at one side. Half-a-dozen steps this way, and we're out in the garden again.'

This proved to be so, and Honeybath and his new companion set out on their short walk. Honeybath, although that latent curiosity in him had been stirred again, wasn't quite easy in his mind. It was really time that he was returning to the house and discovering how Prout was getting on with Edwin. There was also the difficulty of finding a fresh topic of conversation—and one that might at least temporarily relieve Brown from the oppressive compulsion under which he seemed to labour. Brown's fellow residents were a possible resource here. The golf-ball man wouldn't do, since Honeybath had never got round to learning his name. Mr Gaunt of the *misérecordes* and *mains gauches* might serve, but had better be ruled out as himself somewhat morbidly disposed. And Lady Munden belonged to that category of females over sixty which had prompted Brown to his discontented remark on the absence of birds.

'Do you know Colonel Dacre?' Honeybath asked.

'Ah, a useful chap, Dacre.' Brown had paused in his stride. 'Dacre could get a man with a mere revolver at thirty yards. Which takes that amount of doing, you'd be surprised. As for that rifle of his—why, he could make it lethal at a quarter of a mile.'

'Could he, indeed?' Having given this appreciative reply, Honeybath felt prompted to ask, 'Is that how he got Admiral Emery?' But this might sound unsuitably frivolous. 'I suppose,' he offered instead, 'it *could* be useful. Under wartime conditions, that is.'

'Or take a gang.' Mr Brown was walking on. 'You know how it is nowadays. The swamping trick. Learnt from the fuzz themselves, that is. You turn up—at a bank, say—ten or a dozen strong. Suppose they came at us like that. Not in spies but in a bloody battalion. Why, Dacre could pick off half of them before you said six. And a splendid sight it would be.'

Brown had offered this last comment with a sudden malignant glee that Honeybath judged alarming. They were now approaching the perimeter of the park. The park was totally deserted, and so was a stretch of high road immediately beyond. Honeybath found himself wondering whether it had perhaps been just here that Admiral Emery had been innocently wandering when picked off by the colonel—absorbed, with an equal innocence as it might have been, in the charms of a new telescopic sight. Honeybath noticed that Brown's wariness had now increased. He was scanning the road, and the drive leading from it, as if himself under the influence of some fantasy equally absurd.

'And here we are,' Brown said presently. They had come to a halt before *Poseidon urging the Sea-Monster to attack Laomedon*. 'Looks like he was going to clobber somebody, doesn't he? Something nasty gone missing from that right hand, if you ask me. It ought to be restored, it should. I often come and look at him. A wonderful thing, art is. It can say something to a man. Some heathen, I take him to be.'

'The sea-god Neptune,' Honeybath said instructively. 'Homer calls him the Earthshaker.'

'Is that so?' Brown's tone was becomingly respectful. 'Then those would be his sharks, I suppose. I've always supposed they were dogs. Heathen dogs, of course, since dogs don't come like that nowadays. Man-eating sharks, they'll be. And he'd feed you to them, once he'd taken care of you.'

'I must be getting back to the house,' Honeybath said. He spoke a little abruptly, having decided that Brown's imagination was agreeable in short spells only.

'Then I'll leave you to it.' Surprisingly, and perhaps recalling the conventions of those distant days before the shades of the prison house had closed on him, Brown formally doffed his Panama hat. 'I'll just hang around for a bit. I like it here.'

X

THE BIG ROOM that had become Edwin Lightfoot's studio at Hanwell was untenanted. Perhaps Edwin and Prout had themselves gone for a stroll. Honeybath surveyed the place at leisure, and found the general effect reassuring. Whatever labour force was here the equivalent of Mrs Plover must insist on regularly doing its stuff. Edwin had accumulated quite a number of pleasing possessions during the past two years, and a great deal of junk as well. But everything was scrupulously clean, and of disorder there was no more than tends to declare itself in the surroundings of any vigorously creative person. And it looked as if Edwin was in a phase of being such a person. He had a big landscape composition on hand. The pigments were still wet on it, and on a table beside the easel there was a litter of sketches and sketch-books. Unfortunately—for the effort was quite far advanced—Honeybath could see at a glance that Edwin was still painting very badly. It was even possible to infer from the canvas what his current behaviour would be like. 'Jumpy' would be the word for it. Edwin inhabited an agitated universe. So, finally, had Van Gogh. But Edwin's vision of all things turned to flame and light (if he had it) went badly wrong as it was handed on. There were also a few more of the odd portrait affairs around. It was almost —Honeybath reflected—as if these limited and unimportant felicities were by another chap. Honeybath had a dim sense that Edwin might be splitting up.

It also occurred to him, more prosaically, that Edwin might be in the next room, a comfortable apartment to which it would be natural that he and his brother-in-law, perhaps accompanied by Dr Michaelis, had retired for a quiet chat. But this room was untenanted also. Honeybath lingered in it for a couple of minutes, marking the fact that here, too, a great many of Edwin's former possessions were on view. He must have moved in quite a lot of stuff in recent months—perhaps from that depository to which it had been consigned upon the break-up of the Royal Crescent *ménage*. This, in a limited way, seemed a good sign, suggesting that Edwin had come to feel moderately at home in his new environment.

Honeybath returned to the studio, and became aware of Ambrose Prout emerging from the third room in the suite, which was Edwin's bedroom.

'Where is Edwin?' Honeybath asked. 'He's not ill, I hope?' That Edwin was confined to bed seemed the only explanation of Prout's behaviour.

'Oh, no. Edwin's quite all right. Or as right as we'd expect him to be.' Prout added the qualification with his customary gloom. 'He must have missed you. I sent him to look for you in the garden. It struck me a spot of fresh air might do him good.'

Prout was detectably confused—as he might well be when thus discovered in one of his bouts of nosing around. But then Honeybath, too, had been doing something of the sort in the interest of estimating his friend's present nervous condition.

'Have you seen Michaelis?' Honeybath asked.

'Yes—but only briefly. I've arranged that the three of us should have a quiet talk later.'

'Which three of us?'

'You and I and Michaelis, of course. Have you had a look at that thing on the easel, Charles?'

'Yes, I have. It's much the same as what we came on that day we had to have him hospitalized. It's sad.'

'It is, indeed. I couldn't sell that affair to a wandering sheik for a five-pound note.'

'I don't suppose they carry round anything as pitiful as five-pound notes. But you're probably right.'

'It's damned puzzling, Charles. I can't get to the bottom of it.'

'Just what is damned puzzling?' Honeybath was puzzled himself. 'It seems all too clear to me, the decay of Edwin's talent.'

'Oh, nothing, nothing. You're quite right. Absolute decay.' Prout glanced in a curiously furtive way at the door of the studio, as if fearing that its owner might return at an awkward moment. 'I don't know that we should spend long here. There's really nothing to be done.'

'We can at least support Edwin with a little familiar companionship. He can't make much of many of the people in this confounded place.'

'Quite true, quite true. I say—do you think Edwin can be up to some deep game? He's always been as freakish as they come. Capable of anything. That about the burglar, and so on. Quite mad.'

It came to Honeybath that Prout was not merely puzzled. He was also in some abnormal state of excitement. Perhaps it was just something that could be put down to the general atmosphere of Hanwell Court.

'Do you think we should get him away?' Honeybath asked. 'It has been in my head. You remember how he once went off to Italy on his own, and it didn't work? It might be different if he were travelling with a friend. And I could manage to get away for a couple of months myself.'

'It's something to consider—and very generous of you, of course. Something to think over. Perhaps we ought to get away and plan things. Not even bother about that talk with Michaelis.'

'We needn't scurry off just like that.' This new attitude in Prout seemed to Honeybath uncommonly odd, and deserving to be got to the bottom of. It was almost as if something had *happened*. Not for the first time, he was conscious of a strong instinct to distrust Edwin's brother-in-law. 'Ambrose,' he asked sternly, 'are you being quite frank with me?'

'Frank with you?' Alarm rather than reproach had sounded in Prout's voice, and he gave another covert glance at the door. 'There's nothing not to be frank about. But I think, you know, we're meddling with something like a mare's nest. About this affair of the Munden woman. I did have a word with Michaelis about that. And it's blowing over. It seems Edwin has been treating other of the folk here in the same way. Sketching them from memory, that is, with that streak of caricature and in rather ludicrous situations. One or two of them have gone round, and it turns out that the subjects like it. Edwin's an R.A., after all, and his attentions flatter them. I gather he's quite popular.'

'I'm glad to hear it, Ambrose. But the main point . . .' Honeybath broke off. Edwin had entered the studio.

'Charles, so here you are! Ambrose told me about your going to take a look at the orangery. I must have missed you.' Having uttered these words, Edwin Lightfoot embraced Honeybath, stood back, and rubbed his hands with what seemed to be genuine if somewhat febrile pleasure.

Honeybath was about to say, 'I didn't even know there was an orangery.' But thus to expose Prout in prevarication might be to upset Edwin, who was (as forecast) in a jumpy state. It was clear that Prout had sent Edwin on a fool's errand—and that this had been to get him out of his living quarters while Prout did that poking around which now seemed habitual with him. What on earth had the man expected to find in Edwin's bedroom? Did he suspect that it harboured some Paphian girl or rural trollop? And what business of Prout's was it if it did?

Suddenly an extraordinary idea came to Honeybath. It was one of those away-out conjectures that can only visit a man of imaginative endowment. Prout's constant obsession nowadays was with those missing masterpieces of Lightfoot's early period, the existence of which he, and he alone, was obstinately convinced of. Mrs Gutermann-Seuss had proved un-productive—*but what about Lightfoot himself?* Was Edwin crazily hoarding pictures painted long ago—pictures which, if now given to the world through the world's sale-rooms, would vastly enlarge the artist's reputation overnight, to say nothing of vastly enlarging his agent's bank-balance as well? Frequenting Hanwell Court was constraining Honeybath to believe virtually all men mad. Was Ambrose Prout sufficiently mad to believe that Edwin Lightfoot's madness (which he was so constantly asserting) could take so bizarre a form as this? Or *was* it bizarre? With a suddenness equal to that of his first thought on the matter, Honeybath told himself that it was all perfectly possible. One sort of miser irrationally hides away his gold. Mightn't another sort hide away creations of his own far more precious than sovereigns and *louis-d'or*? And wasn't Edwin just the kind of perverse creature of whom such conduct might be predicated? Honeybath was surprised that he hadn't thought all this out before. He would challenge Edwin on it as soon as the two of them were alone together. And this, as it happened, came about almost at once.

'My dear Charles,' Edwin said, 'let me get you a drink. Ambrose, go away.'

'Really, Edwin!' Not unnaturally, Prout was offended by this brisk injunction.

'You and I have had our little chat. It's Charles's turn now. And too many people upset me. And too many people is just what you are. Get lost, old boy. Or try the orangery. Orangery, indeed!'

Producing this childish rudeness, and thus indicating his awareness that he had been imposed upon, seemed to put Edwin in good humour. He chuckled gaily (if also maliciously) as he watched Prout withdraw with what dignity he could.

'Boring chap,' he said, as he rummaged among bottles on a side-table. 'Worse than Melissa herself.' He poured gin liberally into glasses. 'Do you know, I miss Melissa quite a lot. Nobody could imagine themselves missing Ambrose.' He chuckled again—this time on a higher note. 'Impossible not to want to twist his bloody tail at times. And I've found the way to do it. But let's forget about him. I'll show you what I did this morning.'

'To that painting?' As he asked this question, Honeybath glanced towards the easel, and felt embarrassed. He had a notion that Edwin was embarrassed too.

'No, no—just another of those little jokes.' Edwin fished about on another table. 'Have you met a chap here called Dacre?'

'No, I've only heard about him.'

'Very military—very military, indeed. Here he is. I've done him rather after Blake. It's called *The Spiritual Form of the Duke of Wellington surveying the Iberian Peninsula.* Pure nonsense.'

'So it is.' Honeybath studied the latest of Edwin's small extravagances. 'Are you going to show it to him?'

'Oh, yes—Dacre will be rather pleased. Dotty, but a good sort, Dacre. And then I'm going to send it to some exhibition of contemporary drawings that one of those odd councils is proposing to trundle round the country.'

'It strikes me as a little trivial for the purpose.' Honeybath sipped his gin, and resolved that the time had come to tackle Edwin. 'Listen,' he said. 'I want to ask you a straight question. Are you sitting on a number of things you did a long time ago—and that are a good deal more important than most of what you've done since?'

'Now, that's a difficult one, Charles. A really hard question. Quite a philosophical conundrum. Have some more gin.'

'I've barely begun this. And don't talk in riddles. Is it by hiding certain things away that you're contriving to twist Ambrose's bloody tail, as you express it?'

'Ah, now—that's easier. Yes, in a way. But Ambrose isn't important. I'd even call him the quintessence of unimportance. The point is I'm not going to be a freak—not if I can help it. I'm mad, of course. Everybody says that. But not even a madman need be a freak. Keep a joke a joke, I say. All men have their honour. Even artists.' Edwin raised his glass. 'To art, Charles.'

'Edwin, do try . . .'

'You heard what I said.'

'Very well—to art.' Honeybath raised his own glass, and drank. 'Edwin, am I being intrusive? I'd like us to get on well together. Really well, as we used to do. And—do you know?—I've had an idea. I'd terribly like to get back to Italy. You've heard that Piero's *Flagellation* has been returned to Urbino? The thieves seem to have abandoned it in the odd way they do. Shall we go and have a look? We could do Monterchi too. You remember our getting to the lady there when we hadn't so much as a bus fare? We could visit her again.'

'And then to Borgo San Sepolcro for the really great thing.'

'And to Arezzo for San Francesco. Put up in the *Chiavi d'Oro*, and dine in that place in a cellar.' Honeybath broke off in these bold proposals, suddenly aware that Edwin was weeping. It was like being back on square one.

Edwin's sobs died away into a constrained silence. Honeybath didn't know what to say. He had a sense that some essential factor in the situation was eluding him; even that Edwin had hidden it away in that last flood of quirky talk before his abrupt breakdown. Something terrible had happened to Edwin—or at least something bewildering and disorientating. And it was new, or fairly new. It had happened *after* that first occasion upon which he had wept. So it *wasn't* square one. In this seemingly so sheltered place, this funk-hole for the affluent aged and the affluent potty, something undermining had occurred. For Edwin Lightfoot, Hanwell Court was not the Great Good Place. It had turned out—utterly mysteriously—to be the Great Bad Place instead.

There was nothing for it—for the present there was nothing for it—but to play the whole situation down. And it was essential to see young Dr Michaelis at once, and to see him privately rather than in the company of Ambrose Prout as had been proposed. Nor was there any point in longer pretending that Edwin had graduated, as it were, to the position of a mere eccentric at Hanwell Court; to the category in which one could place the golf-ball man or Colonel Dacre or Mr Gaunt of the nasty daggers. Edwin was a man subject to some dreadful sickness of the mind. Or he was an *artist* subject to that. Something had happened to him in that character, and it was something distinct from his now long-established loss of what sports commentators might call his form. This was a very obscure conception, in the light (or darkness) of which it was difficult to see how to act. The simplest step was to secure for Edwin an almost immediate

change of air. Honeybath resolved to cling to that Italian
project.

Even more immediately, it would be a good idea to get
Edwin briefly out of this studio, with its disheartening daub
on the easel and its litter of futile little drawings of Hanwell
Court worthies.

'Let's take a turn in the garden,' Honeybath said, and got
briskly to his feet. 'We can plan the thing during a stroll
there.'

'Plan the thing?' It was quite blankly that Edwin
repeated the words. But he too had got to his feet. He was,
in his way, a very amenable, a suggestible, man.

'We'll fly to Pisa, and hire a car there. It can be waiting
for us, so we can spend our first night in Florence. Unless
one is a rabid Byzantinist, it's the only place from which to
start. We can be in the Carmine or the Pazzi, my boy, forty-
eight hours from now.'

With chat like this, Honeybath got Edwin on the move.
As they were going downstairs they met Ambrose Prout
coming up. Prout passed them without a glance or a word.
He was evidently very much offended still. It was a dis-
pleasing incident. Honeybath was so struck by it that it didn't
occur to him to wonder where the confounded picture-pedlar
was heading for.

XI

I T H A D B E E N a good idea to get out into the open air.
Edwin, although his attention strayed from time to time so
that he walked on in a frowning and muttering abstraction,
did talk rationally about Italy. He didn't fall in explicitly
with Honeybath's plan, but did begin to make random
remarks which seemed to indicate that his mind was moving
in that direction. He was just recollecting (in the sanest
fashion) that there is a thoroughly satisfactory hotel outside
Gubbio when his train of thought was interrupted by the
appearance of Honeybath's earliest Hanwell acquaintance,
Mr Richard Gaunt. Gaunt was nursing what might have
been taken from a distance to be a particularly villainous
Panzerbrecher of gigantic size, but which proved to be
merely a garden fork. The inmates of Hanwell Court, it was
to be observed, were fond of providing themselves with small
tasks in the gardens. Gaunt remembered Honeybath at once.

'My dear sir,' he said, 'I am delighted to see you. Lightfoot, how are you, my dear fellow? I believe I observed you,
Mr Honeybath, in conversation with our friend Brown.'

'Yes, indeed. I'd just met him.' Chatting up Edwin being
hard going, Honeybath welcomed this brief diversion. 'I was
rather curious about him.'

'Not quite from the usual stable, eh? Our mystery man,
I sometimes call him. Retiring fellow. Impossible to get
anything out of him.'

'He seemed to take a certain interest in crime.'

'Very true. Precisely so. And—do you know?—Luxmoore has told me he got the most valuable advice from Brown about rendering the place burglar-proof. Brown concerned himself with the job vigorously. Lightfoot, you recall that?'

This was an unfortunate subject, and Honeybath was rather alarmed by his friend's reaction to it. Edwin, in fact, was tip-toeing round his two companions in a grotesque manner undoubtedly occasioned by revived memories of Flannel Foot. But Mr Gaunt appeared unperturbed by this, being presumably accustomed to Edwin's little ways. He continued to be informative.

'I have myself entertained the conjecture,' he said, 'that Brown was at one time connected with the police. He may even have begun as a bobby on the beat. The highest positions in the constabulary are now, as you know, frequently filled by men coming up from the ranks. There is here an explanation, conceivably, of Brown's somewhat unpolished speech. And now, here is another curious fact about our friend. Lightfoot, I wonder whether you have remarked it? Brown very seldom leaves Hanwell, or even ventures beyond the grounds. But when he does occasionally go away it is for a week or a few nights at a time. And he is collected, and brought back, by a personable young woman driving a discreet but powerful car. It is a vehicle that itself for some reason suggests the police to me.'

'Most interesting,' Honeybath said. Hanwell Court, he reflected, must be a place where a great deal of this close observing of other people's business went on. It wasn't an activity that Edwin would take kindly to having directed upon him.

'But there is something further, my dear Mr Honeybath. It is a circumstance of which I have become aware as a consequence of reading my daily paper with some attention. Those absences of our friend Brown almost invariably coincide with the perpetration, somewhere around the country, of some large-scale robbery of the highly organized sort.'

'Good heavens!' Honeybath, although he had other things to think about than the mysterious Brown, was startled by this striking piece of intelligence. 'You mean you have reason to suppose the man a criminal? Haven't you told the police?'

'Nothing of the kind, my dear sir. Such an idea is obviously absurd. But it has struck me that Brown, before his retirement, was a highly qualified police authority on that sort of thing. Safe-breaking, and so on. A thoroughly scientific business, including the controlled use of high explosives—which brings it almost within the field of my own interest, as you will remember. I take it that when these sensational robberies occur Brown is recalled from retirement in an advisory capacity. But this is mere conjecture, needless to say.'

Honeybath agreed privately that it didn't need saying. Probably everybody at Hanwell Court had some mildly crazy notion about everybody else. This was almost certainly not true of Gubbio. The sooner he got Edwin to Gubbio the better.

But his first task—he reminded himself as he and Edwin took their leave of Gaunt and walked on—was to have that talk with Michaelis and see if any light could be thrown into the darker corners of Edwin's condition. As for Prout, the problem of getting rid of him resolved itself, a little disconcertingly, by Prout's own initiative. Prout had left a scrawled note in the studio, couched in highly offended terms. Edwin had addressed him in such a way that it would be better if they did not again meet for some time. He had no thought of a permanent breach, but an interval for reflection and apology there must be. He proposed to walk to the railway station and catch the next train.

This communication from his brother-in-law failed in

turn to offend Edwin; on the contrary, it induced in him one of those rapid changes of mood in which Honeybath understood that neurotic subjects are prone to indulge. He even capered round the studio before momentarily settling down to sketch Brown from memory. Honeybath didn't doubt that Brown's feet would be represented as swathed in flannel. And this harmless absorption on Edwin's part made it feasible to go off and seek out Dr Michaelis at once.

The Medical Superintendent occupied a curious crypt-like room in the bowels of the building. At some time presumably in the earlier nineteenth century its *décor* and appointments had been pervasively Gothicized by some owner of the house who had grown tired of the Palladian decorum around him. Since a varied paraphernalia of medical science was now disposed around the room the total effect was of a slightly necromantic or even alchemical order. Here, one felt, Paracelsus might have laboured.

But there was nothing of this suggestion about Dr Michaelis himself, or about his more personal goods and chattels. These latter seemed designed to suggest that he was in the full enjoyment of the general affluence diffused throughout Hanwell Court. There were good eighteenth-century watercolours on the walls, Chinese pottery of a plainly authentic sort on a shelf, Hepplewhite chairs that had been sat upon in George Hepplewhite's day. Honeybath, sensitive to these appearances severally, was also capable of a sense that they didn't quite compose or cohere. They reflected nothing in Dr Michaelis himself. He didn't suggest aesthetic feeling; and if he had a concern it was to appear entirely up-to-date.

But he also displayed the same easy manner, correctly short of familiarity, that Honeybath had approved on his previous visit. It was possible to wonder why so capable and alert a young man had relegated himself, so comparatively early in his career, to the medical backwater that caring for the inmates of Hanwell Court must presumably be. Perhaps the pay was particularly good. Or perhaps Michaelis, whom Honeybath recalled as having been rather uncomfortably interested in the psychopathological side of things, himself suffered from some mild disorder in that region. Geronto-philia, it was probably called. The condition of doting upon the aged.

'I didn't regard the business of Lady Munden's portrait as in the least sinister in itself,' Michaelis said. 'A mere foible on your friend Lightfoot's part. We must admit, of course, that he is a man of foibles.'

'No doubt.' Honeybath felt this to be quite a temperate judgement.

'And working in that way must be normal enough with you artists. Easier than simply imagining people.'

'I'd say not.' Honeybath was less satisfied with this last remark, which he even judged rather silly. 'One's first impression of a sitter is much conditioned by types or *schemata* pre-existing in one's own head. The labour comes in peeling away that layer of facile generalization, and arriving at the unique visual phenomenon that is in fact before one.'

'Ah, yes.' Michaelis didn't seem particularly interested in this; indeed, he might almost have not been listening. 'And he has been doing other sketches of the same sort. One or two have been seen by some of his fellow guests, and have gone down quite well. But the activity *might* cause embarrassment. I shall try to persuade Lightfoot to take up something else.'

Although Honeybath judged this to be a good idea in itself, he wasn't too pleased with the notion of Michaelis proposing to boss Edwin around in his vocation.

'Have you noticed,' he asked, 'anything in the quality of

my friend's work? The larger things in oils, I mean. I gather he has been painting a good deal.'

'Indeed, he has. I have encouraged it very strongly. Such things absorb Lightfoot most usefully over long periods of time. When not so engaged he can be—well, a shade tiresome all round. In fact there have been some episodes of real difficulty. But the painting is splendid. I feel he couldn't be doing better. Therapeutically regarded, it is a first-rate occupational resource.'

'I am delighted to hear it.' Honeybath, of course, was nothing of the sort, and he had uttered these words with a severe irony. He was conscious of something undesirably equivocal in the cocksure Medical Superintendent's role. But this no doubt proceeded from the fact that the place discreetly played down its function as in part at least a receptacle for mildly loopy persons. 'What I was curious to know,' Honeybath went on (easing off only a little on the irony), 'is whether you have examined any of the individual paintings with any attention. Would you say they were good, or bad?'

'Oh, good. Decidedly good, many of them. Most interesting. Tell me, Mr Honeybath—did Lightfoot lose his mother in infancy; and, if so, was she almost at once succeeded by a stepmother?'

'My dear sir, I have no idea whatever. And I cannot imagine . . .'

'There has been one very interesting landscape painting. It is dominated by a large tree; one may say a sheltering and sustaining tree. Only it is impossible quite to tell whether it is *one* tree. It might almost be *two* trees, with their several trunks at once distinct and confused. A really beautiful picture. I made some careful notes on it. Tell me, do you know whether in infancy Lightfoot ever had an alarming experience with a cat?'

'Again I have no idea.' Honeybath's astonishment and indignation mounted. 'Nor, I imagine, has he.'

'Indeed not. It would be entirely a matter of repressed memory. But there it was—in one of the pictures. Ostensibly the shadow cast by a man haymaking. But in fact the perfect silhouette of a cat.'

'Most enlightening.' Honeybath had a dim memory of nonsense of this sort being rendered persuasive by the formidable creative endowment of Sigmund Freud. Michaelis, on the other hand, was no artist. Carousing cardinals in red, or darling puppies in a basket, would be very much the same thing to him as *Las Meninas* or *The Burial of Count Orgaz*. He'd search them all indifferently for evidence of the traumata of childhood.

'And at first,' Michaelis was saying, 'it wasn't easy to get Lightfoot going. He seemed to have taken against painting. And he'd wander around the place in an agitated way, often pretending to be somebody else.'

'Ah, yes. It's a kind of game he plays. He associates it with charades.'

'Charades. Thank you.' Michaelis turned to his desk and made a rapid note. 'As I was saying, I had difficulty in getting Lightfoot to settle down with his materials. It was the same for a time with the elder Miss Pinchon and her basket-work. But, of course, we have our techniques. There are the resources of science.'

'Good heavens!' Honeybath was outraged. 'Do you mean that you drugged or doped Lightfoot into labouring at work he no longer had any spontaneous prompting to?'

'Nothing of the sort, Mr Honeybath.' Michaelis appeared shocked in his turn. 'Apart from a few reliable psychotropic drugs, I view all chemicotherapy as undesirably hazardous. Irreversible side-effects may always turn up. Not that related hazards may not attend other techniques. I had to break off with Lightfoot, as a matter of fact. Happily, the habit had been substantially restored. He has continued to paint, one may say, pretty well by rote.'

'And uncommonly badly. Dr Michaelis, I am constrained to say that I don't care for the sound of all this at all.' Honeybath felt that the time had come to stand up and be counted on his friend's behalf. 'And I may add that I have been discussing future plans with Lightfoot. We intend to visit Italy together very shortly. There will be details to settle about his possible later return to Hanwell, and so on. But that can readily be arranged, and I shall take it upon myself to discuss the matter with Brigadier Luxmoore.' Honeybath recalled with some satisfaction that Dr Michaelis was no more than a second-in-command at Hanwell Court. 'And I am sure,' he added with grim formality, 'that Lightfoot will always be grateful to you for the interest you have shown in his work. May I ask whether you told him about your remarkable discovery of the cat?'

'We had a number of instructive discussions, of course.' Michaelis was entirely unruffled and urbane. 'I hope you intend to lunch with us?'

'Lightfoot and I are going to take a short walk on the downs.' Honeybath thus announced as a fact what had only just come into his head. 'We shall pick up a sandwich at an inn. And I shall make our travel arrangements the moment I get back to town.' For the moment, at least, Honeybath was feeling strongly anti-Hanwell. Like the dreadless Angel in Milton's poem, he was all for turning his back on those proud towers, and could almost have wished them to swift destruction doomed. He had done wrong ever to dump Edwin in the place.

'I envy you your foreign trip,' Michaelis said amiably. 'Italy is a wonderful country. A veritable cradle of the arts.'

'Quite so. And of the sciences, too, for that matter.'

Honeybath added this with the notion, equally amiable, of patching up some sort of *concordat* with this tiresome mad-doctor. 'But I have taken up too much of your valuable time.'

'Not at all. I am always at your disposal, my dear sir.'

On this note of decent amenity the interview ended.

XII

ONE WOULD SCARCELY expect Mrs Gutermann-
Seuss to re-enter the story. She had appeared to be a
write-off so far as Ambrose Prout's devoted quest for early
Lightfoots was concerned. The wretched woman, although
the widow of one formerly eminent in Prout's own trade,
had not known the difference between a genuine Lightfoot
of that golden lustre and a forgery of the most pitiful sort.
Or so it had appeared. And so Honeybath had thought until,
on reaching Rome in Edwin Lightfoot's company, he had
found a letter from Prout awaiting him at his hotel.

It was a letter, in the first place, exuding forgiveness and
reconciliation, and it continued in a vein of virtual euphoria
which explained itself when the name of Gutermann-Seuss
hove into view. There had been some gross misconception—
a consequence of Prout's not actually having interviewed the
lady himself—and he had been shown that objectionable
curiosity when the real thing actually existed in the next
room.

And it *was* the real thing : small and very simple—in fact
no more than a bunch of zinnias in a porcelain vase. But at
a mere glance it announced itself for what it was. Prout was
now its fortunate owner, since he had purchased it (probably
to an eventual modest advantage) on the spot. He would be
most grateful if Honeybath would tell Edwin about it; even
sound Edwin for any recollection of it he had. Not that
establishing a strict provenance was essential when it was a

question of so unchallengeably authentic a thing. And
Edwin, of course, would probably *not* remember it, since his
memory was quite as much in decay as the rest of him. It
was just possible—Prout added in a postscript—that this
excellent Mrs Gutermann-Seuss might harbour something
further of Edwin's, since her possessions lay around the
Brighton house in great profusion and confusion. But Prout
would go easy on this possibility for a time, since it would be
impolitic to let the lady feel there was too much in the wind.

Honeybath hesitated for some time about showing this
letter to his friend, although he was clearly intended to do
so. There was nothing in the deal for Edwin, and of course
no reason why there should be; nor would Edwin be at all
concerned about that aspect of the matter. He might, however, be upset by the mere fact of an early picture turning
up. Hadn't he reacted in an agitated and equivocal way to
the suggestion that he might himself be sitting on a clutch
of the things? But in the end Honeybath did hand the letter
over. That it contained an unflattering estimate of Edwin's
mental and physical condition didn't matter very much, since
Edwin managed to delight at once in declaring himself mad
and in making fun of his brother-in-law's conviction that he
was so.

Edwin declared that he had never heard of Gutermann-
Seuss, and that even if the existence of this person at a
former time were proved to him, he would still dispute the
probability of his having left a widow. (It was a sign,
Honeybath thought, of a substantial recovery of nervous
tone on Edwin's part that he talked nonsense like this.) As
for zinnias, he had no memory of ever painting such things,
and he doubted whether he would recognize a zinnia if one
were shown to him now. It was quite possible, of course,
that Melissa had once stuck a bunch of flowers in front of
him and that he had gone to work on it. Perhaps he had

pretended that he was Fantin-Latour or even some piddling Dutchman. They'd used to play, hadn't they, games like that?

Honeybath agreed that they had, and Prout's letter was mentioned no more. The Italian trip was proving quite a success. Edwin was frequently depressed, and occasionally excited and bizarre. He advanced odd reasons for visiting one place and avoiding another. Assisi was dangerous because wolves still came prowling down from Monte Subasio, and turned nasty when they failed to find their old chum. Perugia was impossible because even the clothes of all those charming youths in Perugino's paintings were impregnated with the smell of chocolate. It wasn't always easy to tell when Edwin was producing fun and when the detritus of a disordered imagination. And this conversation, particularly of an anecdotal and reminiscent sort, was difficult to follow because he had a fondness for nicknames that came and went like quicksilver. Who were Soggy Sabrina and Narky Ned and Signor Cipolla? Honeybath felt he was expected to know—which he certainly did not. But at least Edwin's intermittent clowning never exhibited itself in front of works of art. It might have been said that these turned him sane at once. Nor, before them, did he beweep his outcast state, or envy this man's art and that man's scope. As the little tour went on Honeybath became more and more convinced that he had hit upon the right thing. It was Italy that was the Great Good Place.

This view of the matter took a severe dent, indeed, when the two artists ran into Melissa. This happened in Rome in the Sans Souci, a fact making the coincidence a shade less remarkable than it would otherwise have been. The gastronome (if not sybarite) lurking in Lightfoot had brought the two men to this celebrated place of refection, and Melissa was remembering it from earlier years when she and her husband had presumably been on better terms. Honeybath was half-way through something called Danilo's Dream, and Edwin was discussing a Miracolo San Bruno, when Melissa simply walked across the restaurant and stood planted before them. Her presence in Rome remained only vaguely explained, but it was to be presumed that Deep Meditation had rather let her down, and that she had decided on a spell of High Living instead.

'They look distinctly out of place,' Melissa said, as she glanced from one to the other. 'Not properly dressed for this place at all. They might be Germans. Or even Americans.'

'Melissa, sit down.' Honeybath had frequently uttered these words equally firmly in the past. The effect of Melissa was slightly less devastating when she was constrained to direct address. 'We're delighted to see you,' he added on a conciliatory note. 'I hope you're going to dine with us.' It would be well worth a couple of thumping lies, he thought, if Melissa could be persuaded to take a seemly view of this encounter. He couldn't quite think of what was the Italian equivalent of *le haut ton* or *la crème de la crème*. But they were presumably surrounded by it in this elegant establishment.

'I meant to go to the White Elephant,' Melissa said, a little discontentedly. She had sat down. 'But I lost my way.'

'Ah, the White Elephant.' Honeybath didn't in fact know the White Elephant. It sounded like a pub (but in this he was mistaken), which would have been more his style. 'I expect we can find something to suit you. I don't know who Danilo was. But his Dream is at least no Nightmare.'

This was jocularity on the nervous side. Here was Edwin contented and enjoying himself; definitely to be described as on the mend. But Melissa's irruption was unlikely to fortify the convalescent process.

'Penne Karlof,' Melissa said, decisively if mysteriously.

'*Si, si, Signora.*' Edwin had jumped to his feet, draped his table napkin over his arm, and was inclining his head respectfully over his wife's shoulder—with a hand holding an imaginary pencil poised over an imaginary scribbling block. Edwin, all too plainly, was putting on one of his turns. It was a critical moment. Honeybath, however, had come to exercise a considerable degree of authority over his travelling companion, and he succeeded in repressing him now. Melissa watched the process with an appraising eye.

'Is Edwin all right?' she asked.

'Of course Edwin's all right.'

'Ambrose is anxious about him.' Melissa might have been talking about a domestic pet, or a child still of years too tender to understand that it was a topic of debate. 'Ambrose says his memory is entirely gone, and that he would be totally unreliable in anything he said about himself. Ambrose believes that distressing physical symptoms are sure to follow. Are his sphincters still tolerably in order?'

'Melissa, dear, your sense of humour can be deplorable. Do be serious.' Honeybath had glanced apprehensively at Edwin, who might well react unfavourably to these outrageous remarks. But Edwin had achieved a rapid withdrawal within himself, and seemed to be paying no attention to either of his companions. He continued, however, to be appreciatively aware of the Miracolo San Bruno.

'Very well.' Melissa paused to brief a waiter on her need of Penne Karlof; presumably it was a dish claiming to be as light as feathers. 'Ambrose has found three early paintings. I suppose you've heard that.'

'Three!'

'All from the lumber room of some dreadful old woman in Brighton. Or so he says. I don't believe she exists. But, if she does, I suppose the pictures were her lawful property. They're Ambrose's now. I think it's very odd.'

'Are you insinuating, Melissa, that your brother isn't being quite straight about them?' It was in a tone of severe disapproval that Honeybath asked this. He was coming less and less to care for Prout, but he judged Melissa's line to be scandalously unsisterly.

'I think there should be something in it for us. And haven't I to protect Edwin's interests? He is my husband, you know.'

'An ill-favoured thing, sir, but mine own.' Edwin produced this Shakespearian thought without the slightest appearance of emerging from his abstraction. The effect of this was disturbing, to say the least.

'Have you seen these pictures?' Honeybath asked. Although reluctant to continue this conversation on its present terms, he felt a very strong curiosity in the matter.

'No, I haven't. Ambrose refused to show them to me. But I'll tell you a funny thing. Just before I came away, I went to see him on some business of quite a different sort. He didn't so much as want to let me into his flat. But I insisted, and found a man with him whom he simply refused to introduce. It was extremely unmannerly. I hate bad manners.' Melissa made this perhaps surprising claim emphatically. 'So I said to this person quite firmly : "Who are you?" And he told me his name was Michaelis, and that he knew Edwin. He seemed quite embarrassed. Of course the name conveyed nothing to me. So I just left some papers with Ambrose, and came away. But I thought it funny, as I said. I don't know why I thought it funny, but I did.'

'Hilarious.' Edwin had suddenly become attentive to his companions in the most normal-seeming way. 'Michaelis, Melissa, is a leech they keep around Hanwell to paw people's tummies and peer inside their heads. A well-meaning chap,

I'd say, and quite splendidly without a scrap of aesthetic sense. I suppose your brother has hopes of him, and had got him along in order to chat him up. Naturally they'd be a bit embarrassed when you poked in.'

'What do you mean by saying Ambrose has hopes of him?' Melissa demanded. 'I don't understand you.'

'Ambrose would like to see me shut up good and proper, and feels the chap might sign on the dotted line. He regards me as an expensive nuisance, Ambrose does.' Edwin offered these shocking opinions with what seemed perfect good-humour, and Honeybath found it impossible to tell whether he was in fact startled by the information his wife had produced. 'I expect he had a preliminary go at it the last time he came down to Hanwell, just before Charles and I took off from the place.'

'My dear Edwin,' Honeybath said, 'for goodness sake don't start imagining things. Michaelis has been your medical adviser—at least in a vague sort of way. It would be grossly improper of him to hold the sort of confabulations you suggest with a person who is no more than your brother-in-law.'

'Then, Charles, what *was* it in aid of? Ambrose's barging in on Michaelis at Hanwell is one thing. But this affair at Ambrose's own flat is a most unlikely get-together. It certainly wasn't for the purpose of having a friendly drink. Incidentally, let's get Melissa some champagne. She deserves it.'

Honeybath called for the champagne. He didn't like Edwin's curiously relaxed manner a bit, and moreover he was unable himself to find a motive that could have prompted the odd conference Melissa had stumbled into. In a groping kind of way he connected it with the possibly mythical Mrs Gutermann-Seuss and the turning up of those three early Lightfoots. What if a cache of the things really did exist, but was perhaps still Edwin's own property and concealed somewhere at Hanwell Court? He had himself actually sounded Edwin about something like this, and received what he dimly remembered as an evasive reply. And no further light on it had emerged during the present Italian trip, perhaps because it had been Honeybath's line to consign Hanwell and any mystery that might be connected with it to at least a temporary limbo. Now he found himself intuitively convinced that Edwin's very ease of manner was ominous; that it was a disguise that might blow away at any moment and land him again with a companion who had been given occasion to be seriously disturbed. He cursed this luckless visit to the Sans Souci—or alternatively Melissa's incompetent inability to find her way to the White Elephant. He was even sufficiently upset to think of breaking up the party before the champagne was finished. He distrusted the effect of the stuff on Melissa, for one thing. She was a woman who easily got tiddly (which was the correct vulgar word for it), and if she and Edwin then got across one another there might be the most distressing scene.

But he restrained himself, and nothing of the sort happened. Melissa appeared puzzled rather than challenging. Edwin returned to his former abstraction, and finished the evening with a composure that was wholly commendable. He was like a man relieved of tension because some power of decision has been restored to him.

This last impression was soon to explain itself. The two men returned to their hotel in the hair-raising fashion inseparable from a nocturnal ride across Rome in a taxi-cab.

'I'm going to pack,' Edwin said, when he had arrived outside his bedroom door.

'My dear Edwin, you're forgetting. We're going to spend three more days in Rome.'

'You may be. I'm going home.'

'What do you mean—home?' This was not, perhaps, a tactful question, since Edwin's only home now was the curious establishment in which Honeybath had persuaded him to domesticate himself.

'Hanwell, of course. I'm going to clear things up there.'

'You mean you've decided to move out?' It was Honeybath's conviction now that this was the best course that Edwin could adopt. He was uneasy, all the same.

'I suppose so.'

'Of course I'll come back with you, Edwin. Perhaps I can give you a hand over the next few weeks. There will be quite a lot to consider.'

'I'd rather you didn't break off your holiday, Charles.'

'Nonsense! It has been *our* holiday. And I've enjoyed it.'

Honeybath spoke robustly. But in this he was only echoing Edwin's own tone. Edwin was being quite as commanding about this return to England as his friend had been about quitting it. There could be no doubt that the Italian interlude was over. At noon next day they were a few thousand feet above Mont Blanc. They parted at Heathrow, Edwin having revealed a disinclination to be returned to Hanwell Court as it were under convoy.

Back in London, Honeybath resolved to let a couple of days pass before contacting Edwin by telephone. For Edwin, his resolution taken, seemed reasonably composed, and he might be irritated by any too obtrusive determination to keep on holding his hand.

But on the third morning Honeybath called Hanwell Court, and asked if he might be put through to Mr Lightfoot. The request produced a moment's odd silence, and he repeated it.

'I'm afraid not,' a voice then said. It was the kind of voice that, normally, is briskly secretarial. But on this occasion it sounded not so much at a loss as on the verge of panic. 'Mr Lightfoot isn't available,' the voice said. The effect of this was of a seizing of the first familiar formula to hand.

'He has left Hanwell Court?' It sounded to Honeybath as if there had been an awkward bust-up and Edwin had departed in a stink of sulphur.

'Well, yes in a sense. I'm terribly sorry, Mr Honeybath.' The agitated young woman at the other end of the line appeared to take a deep breath. 'Mr Lightfoot died last night. He was found drowned this morning.'

XIII

THE STRANGE MANNER of Edwin Lightfoot's death
was eventually to strike an enterprising journalist as good
for a write-up in a Sunday paper; and this elevating of the
fatality to the status of a spurious 'sensation' was eventually
to have a wholly unexpected sequel of a genuinely sensational
sort. But that lay a little in the future. When Honeybath
reached Hanwell Court the atmosphere (as might have been
foretold) was all reticence and a sustained decorum. It was
true that there were several policemen around, but Honeybath felt at once that they were disposed (in the current
phrase) to present a low profile to the affair. One of them,
although in plain clothes and known as plain Mr Adamson,
suggested himself as of higher rank than a rural constabulary
might have been thought able to turn on at short notice.
Mr Adamson seemed very willing to confer with Honeybath
without much inquiring into his standing in the matter.
Honeybath, he might have been conceding, was a person of
consequence and to be deferred to. And as Honeybath had
lately been travelling on the Continent with the dead man
anything he had to say might be of help in clearing up any
element of the mysterious that might conceivably lurk in
this distressing occurrence.

'These things do tend to happen late at night,' Adamson
said. 'A man dines well, and so on. Then he has bad luck,
and the accident happens. If he has very bad luck, as in Mr
Lightfoot's case, the accident is unhappily fatal.'

'Quite so.' Honeybath paused for a moment, and decided that there had been an implication in this that must be challenged. 'Only there is no reason to suppose that Lightfoot "dined well"—or not in the sense you suggest. He could be a convivial man in congenial company. But I doubt whether there is much conviviality at Hanwell Court. You have to think of Lightfoot sitting at his own small table, eating his meal, and drinking a glass—or perhaps a couple of glasses—of wine. Certainly not as living it up.'

'He was a habitually temperate man?'

'He certainly wasn't a drunk.' Honeybath felt considerable indignation at the line Mr Adamson was developing. 'Am I to understand that he was observed by anybody last night in an intoxicated condition?'

'I haven't heard of anything of the sort so far.'

'Then the whole speculation is gratuitous.'

'Fair enough, Mr Honeybath.' Adamson wasn't at all ruffled. 'But you must remember our position. There are more or less routine questions which the coroner may feel it his duty to raise. And we have to credibilize what happened, if I may put it that way. A perfectly sober man might stumble into a pond like that in the dark. But it's hard to believe that a perfectly sober man wouldn't simply climb out again. You've seen the pond, Mr Honeybath?'

'No, I have not. I happened never to have made my way there, although I have visited Hanwell Court on a number of occasions. I suppose it is the salt-water pond in which a woman called Lady Munden amuses herself by growing or cultivating seaweed?'

'Just so—and a singularly futile hobby, it seems to me. But it appears that the lady has had considerable success in acclimatizing—if that's the word—various exotic varieties. I had a man from a Marine Institute looking into it a couple of hours ago. *Fucus giganteus*, he said, which is the biggest of the lot. Stems as thick as a cable. But what proved really treacherous and fatal was bull-head Kelp. It seems that the Red Indians make fishing-lines of it. But I still don't believe that a quite sober man could have tangled himself up in it.'

'That's what happened?' Not unnaturally, Honeybath was appalled by this revelation. 'Edwin—Lightfoot—died that way?'

'Yes, indeed. The body had to be cut out of the stuff.'

'Good God!' There had been occasions upon which Honeybath had indulged a vein of macabre fantasy about possible sudden death at Hanwell: one of the Misses Pinchon going the way of Admiral Emery at a touch on Colonel Dacre's trigger; Mr Gaunt running amuck with a poisoned dagger; even some harmless inmate wandering into the maze and never being seen again. But Lady Munden's saline pool as a hazard had never occurred to him.

'But do you know?' Mr Adamson was saying. 'There came into my head this morning something I'd once read about the poet Shelley.'

'About Shelley? What can Shelley have to do with it?' Asking this reasonable question, Honeybath was confirmed in his suspicion that Adamson emanated from the superior echelons of the police, among whom there may be supposed individuals conversant with polite literature.

'Shelley took it into his head on some occasion that it would be quite nice just to drown.'

'I doubt whether it was a view he maintained to the end of his life.'

'One supposes not.' Adamson clearly took this reference without effort. 'Well, Shelley simply lay down on the bottom of a pool and calmly stayed put. I forget how he was rescued. But it must have been a difficult thing to do—just lying there quietly. If he'd been in Lady Munden's pond, of course, *Fucus giganteus* and Bull-head Kelp would have helped.'

'Great heavens! You don't suggest . . .'

'Just wriggle into the stuff, and you wouldn't quickly wriggle out again. Mr Honeybath, would you describe your friend as of melancholic or depressive temperament?'

'You had better ask Dr Michaelis.' Honeybath at once thought better of this evasive reply. 'I'd say that Edwin Lightfoot went up and down a good deal. "Cyclothymic", I believe, is the technical term.'

'And how was he during your visit to Italy together? Would you say he was under any particular stresses and strains?'

'He had been, undoubtedly. He was dissatisfied with his work.'

'With his painting, that is? Had he reason to be? Objective reason, I mean, such as another painter like yourself would judge well-founded. Or was it a matter of his having set himself an impossibly high standard, and being dejected because he couldn't attain to it?'

'His work was undoubtedly deteriorating.' Honeybath had been a little surprised by Adamson's string of questions. But there could be no doubt about what prompted them. Indeed, Adamson now came out with it forthrightly.

'Mr Honeybath, you will see that here is a question I have to ask. Were you ever apprehensive of Mr Lightfoot's taking his own life?'

'Yes—but only as something, so to speak, on the verge of possibility. Moreover I think others may have entertained the same thought. But as an explanation of Lightfoot's death under the circumstances in which it has taken place, suicide appears to me quite ludicrous. Can we conceivably believe, Mr Adamson, that he climbed into a comparatively shallow pool, and there so deliberately entangled himself in all that abominable stuff as to ensure that it would be beyond his power to free himself were he prompted to do so? It is the sheerest nonsense, and we don't make it less so by talking about Shelley.' Honeybath hadn't finished uttering these last words before regretting them as discourteous rather than merely tart, and when Adamson's response was a very genuine laugh he was considerably relieved. 'But I take it,' he added, 'that you're thinking once more about that coroner?'

'And his jury, Mr Honeybath. But I don't really expect much trouble ahead. This and that will be canvassed; and it will become clear that nobody knows or is going to know; and these worthy people, after being dragged away from their desks and counters for the better part of a day, will bring in what is called an open verdict, and go home to their teas and suppers.'

'You don't think there's anything more to find out?' It seemed to Honeybath that Adamson's last remarks, although they established him yet more firmly in that superior echelon, had been on the cavalier side.

'Well, of course, this or that may turn up. To go back, for instance, to my first very tentative conjecture. It's possible that the post mortem may disclose in the body whatever it is that is left there after the breakdown of a good deal of alcohol. But, even so, I'd hope that nothing much need be made of it. One always hopes that these things won't attract vulgar curiosity or be made a thing of in the newspapers. And I know Mr Lightfoot's work, as it happens, and regard him as a man of very real eminence. I think we can manage the press.'

'I'm told there have been several reporters here already this morning.'

'Oh, yes—and their brief reports will appear. Beyond that, they can be managed.'

'Managed?' Honeybath felt this to be somehow a mildly scandalous word.

'They come along, you know, asking for information one isn't in the least obliged to give them. But one plays them on an easy line. "Ah, yes," one says. "But I don't think there is really much for you in *that*. But listen to *this*." And one hands them out a good lead on some hardened villain. It's all part, my dear Mr Honeybath, of a policeman's prime duty to protect the respectable classes.'

'I see.' This urbanely ironical stuff was not alien to Honeybath's taste, but he didn't care for it hard up against Edwin's death. 'Perhaps I haven't made it clear,' he said firmly, 'that Edwin Lightfoot was my oldest friend. We had grown a little apart, as it happens, a few years ago, but then came together again. As you do know, the last weeks of his life were spent in my company. It is fair to say that I feel a certain duty to his memory.'

'A duty, Mr Honeybath?' Adamson was entirely serious again.

'And I'd wish, as far as it can be done, to clarify the circumstances of his death. There is one possibility, is there not, that we have failed to discuss so far?'

'Foul play.' Adamson smiled faintly. 'The papers are going to report that "the police do not suspect foul play." I sometimes wonder how many criminals are gullible enough to believe it.'

'Then you *do* suspect foul play?'

'I acknowledge its possibility.'

'But not its probability, Mr Adamson? That seems fair enough. There are unlikely, I suppose, to be any hardened villains, as you call them, at Hanwell Court.'

'That is possibly true.' The faint irony had returned to Adamson. 'But murder, as it happens, is commonly an amateur affair. Professional criminals have been taking to it rather ominously, it is true, in recent years. But in the main homicide continues to be—shall we say?—a very special sort of crime.' Adamson paused for a moment. 'However, Mr Honeybath, it is not in our character as philosophers that we are conversing at the moment. Have you any reason whatever to believe that Mr Lightfoot was murdered? If you have, please tell me about it.'

'I have none. I can certainly say that I have none. But my mind is not entirely at ease, all the same.' Honeybath paused in his turn. He knew that what he had in his head was so vague and shadowy—and so remote from any of the darker forms of crime—that he might stumble badly if he embarked on it now. 'Edwin Lightfoot was the most honourable of men. To be involved in anything shady would have been wholly alien to his nature. But in these last months of his life he was, I believe, being practiced upon in a manner that remains quite obscure to me. What I have in mind—only very obscurely in mind— may be wholly unrelated to the manner of his death. And I simply can't embark on this now. To do so might be to involve entirely innocent people in senseless and fantastic suspicion. I must think about it—and even a little cast about on my own. I am afraid that I can say no more to you.'

Honeybath had made this speech with an irrational sense that it was going to get him into instant trouble; that he was liable to be sternly admonished about his duty as a liege and a citizen to come clean in the interest of the Queen's peace. That sort of thing. So he was surprised when this formidable policeman didn't take that line at all.

'I quite understand you, Mr Honeybath,' Adamson said. 'Perhaps we may have another talk on a later occasion. It may even be that you would wish to communicate with me rapidly. In that case, it would be quite in order to by-pass the county constabulary.' Adamson brought out a notebook, scribbled in it, tore out the leaf, and handed it to Honeybath. 'This would be the telephone number.' For a fraction of a second Adamson hesitated. 'Mr Honeybath,' he then said, 'you are a wholly reliable man. In confidence, then, let me say that it will put you in immediate contact with my office in New Scotland Yard.' Adamson smiled fleetingly. 'I have strayed in here, you see, from the Metropolitan Police Office. And I'm bound to say the local bobbies are being very nice about it. And—what's more important—very discreet as well.'

XIV

B UT HONEYBATH TOO had strayed in. One can't visit
a corpse, and as yet there wasn't even any word of a funeral.
It would be Melissa who would have to be consulted about
that, and about the various practical dispositions to be made
thereafter. Melissa hadn't yet showed up, but when she did
she would either take charge of things or nominate persons
to do the job for her. The Lightfoots hadn't been divorced;
they hadn't even been separated to any legal effect. Honeybath thought it probable that, had it ever occurred to Edwin
to make a will, he might find himself appointed as an
executor. Meanwhile, he was only a concerned old friend.
He had meant what he said, however, when he had told
Adamson that he was prompted to remain on the scene
for a time and a little cast about on his own. But Hanwell
Court wasn't a hotel, so he couldn't simply march up to
a desk and book a room. On the other hand he was sufficiently well known to Brigadier Luxmoore, Dr Michaelis
and others as the dead man's intimate friend to make it
seem perfectly natural and proper that he should come and
go for a time, and render a general effect of doing a little
tidying up. He decided to walk over to the local pub, secure
himself a couple of nights' accommodation there, and then
return to Hanwell Court. Considerable mystery *did* attach
to the manner of Edwin's death, and he had an obstinate
feeling that certain apparently unrelated facts which he
alone was in possession of might turn out to be involved in

the horrible business after all. He was departing up the drive, and had come in view of *Poseidon urging the Sea-Monster to attack Laomedon*, when it occurred to him that he hadn't yet viewed what his imagination was hinting to him ought to be called the scene of the crime. It may have been the Sea-Monster itself—a sufficiently hideous aquatic phenomenon—that thus put Lady Munden's opprobrious pool in his head. He had a general notion of where it lay. He now turned aside in search of it.

Quite probably, he thought, it would still be under some sort of guardianship by the police, who would be concerned to keep it from intrusion until certain that no more enlightenment was to be dredged from it. His approach, therefore, was made with circumspection. But he proved to be wrong in his persuasion. The pool was deserted. He felt this to be part of the general disposition of the police to play down Edwin's death. It was a curious feeling to have, since it couldn't in any way be averred that Edwin was being cheated of something. Yet he had convinced himself —he recognized this now—that Adamson at least wasn't pleased by what had happened at Hanwell Court. It seemed impossible to make sense of this. Yet the idea clung to him.

It was quite a large pool. Some parts of it were comparatively clear, and others were clotted and crammed with the stringy or ramifying or bulbous or pulpy stuffs which were Lady Munden's peculiar devotion. Lady Munden, he told himself, might be regarded as the Nereïd of this nasty flood. She might rise out of it at any moment, waving a conch or other symbol of her watery nature. Or she might be glimpsed in the depths, like Shelley—only *in twisted braids of Lillies knitting the loose train of her amber-dropping hair.* That was Milton's Sabrina, Honeybath told himself as he began to round the pool, and he wondered what on earth (or in water) had brought this snatch of verse within his recollection. Then he remembered that Edwin had obscurely referred to somebody as 'soggy Sabrina'. It was quite possibly Lady Munden that he had meant.

At the far end of the pool there stood an undistinguished pavilion-like structure, with an extension glassed in on three sides. It recalled the kind of shelter to be found scattered along some seaside esplanades. The people who had provided Lady Munden with her pool were probably in that line of business too, and had added this affair to boost their bill. It wasn't at all congruous with the general elegance of the grounds of Hanwell Court. Honeybath was noting this fact with disapproval when he discovered that the shelter was occupied. The man seated in it—and surveying the scene of the late fatality with a philosophic eye—proved to be the socially anomalous Mr Brown. Honeybath had failed to identify him immediately because he was not, on this occasion, wearing a Panama hat.

'Ah, good day to you, my dear Honeybath!' This robust and cordial greeting, although perhaps a shade too familiar in the form of words chosen, came from Brown with quite agreeable effect. Honeybath made a suitable reply. Brown, he felt, ought to be encouraged in his laudably pertinacious attempts to recover the manners and assumptions native to him before the unhappy period of his incarceration. (Honeybath had finally come down on the side of what might be called the luckless-financier interpretation of Brown.)

'Would you say, now, that the Sargasso Sea looks like that?' As he asked this question, Brown waved a hand over Lady Munden's saline pool.

'There may well be a certain resemblance.' Honeybath, although his mood was sombre, managed to be amused by this question. 'I have never seen the Sargasso Sea.'

'Wonderful yarns I used to read about it as a boy.

Spanish galleons and the like stuck in it as thick as flies on fly-paper and mouldering away for centuries.'

'Ah, yes! I read that sort of thing too. An imaginative conception. I believe the actual thing is fairly patchy, and that the possibility of craft being permanently stuck in it was disproved early in the present century.' Honeybath felt that this was too much in his informative vein. 'But one likes to think of those stranded Armadas. Serving a kind of maritime life sentence, one might say.'

'Just that.' Brown took this analogy—prompted by Honeybath's recollection of his curious interest in such matters—entirely in his stride. 'But your friend Lightfoot,' he said briskly. '*He* got stuck. I've been sitting here thinking about it. A sad event, Honeybath. A very sad event, indeed. And happening just before his exhibition, too.'

'His exhibition?' Honeybath was puzzled. 'What was that?'

'What he told me about one day, shortly before the two of you went abroad together. That there was soon to be an introspective exhibition . . .'

'A retrospective exhibition?'

'That was it. Of everything he'd ever done, he said. At the Tate Gallery, down near Imperial Chemicals.'

'Ah, yes.' Honeybath avoided any tone of surprise. Poor Edwin must have been in a particularly freakish mood to spin the imperfectly informed Brown such a tale.

'And then he tumbled into this nasty stuff. Or did he?'

'Or *did* he?' This time, Honeybath was really startled.

'It was done to him, if you ask me. Nobody will believe it, of course—but that's my view. Somebody was looking after him. Don't ask me why—but these things happen. Tipped him in, and then used a pole, likely enough.'

'A pole?' Honeybath hadn't thought of this particular horror.

'With a forked end, I'd say. Pushed him down and pushed him down, until the poor bugger was well tangled up. It sickens me, it does.'

'I'm not surprised.' What sickened Honeybath was the thought of this deplorable man sitting here almost hard upon Edwin's death, and entertaining himself with such a revolting fantasy. Or was it a fantasy? Honeybath himself had simply not got round to envisaging in detail just how Edwin had been made away with—if made away with he had been.

'But who done it?' Brown asked. 'Who did it, that's to say.' Brown paused with evident satisfaction on this grammatical nicety. 'Answer me that.'

'I don't think I can, Mr Brown.' Honeybath hesitated. 'Have you any specific suspicion yourself?'

'There are those up there at the house that are in a fair panic, Honeybath. I'll say no more than that. An inside job, it has been.' Brown gazed darkly in the direction of the serene facade of Hanwell Court. 'I've an eye for such things that seldom goes wrong, although I say it myself. Just keep your own eyes skinned, Honeybath, and you'll see what you'll see.'

'I'll do what I can. But now I fear I must leave you.' Honeybath had had enough of being Honeybathed by Brown. He gave a firm nod and walked away.

Rounding Poseidon, he asked himself a new and alarming question. Was the extraordinary Brown perhaps a homicidal maniac? Had he senselessly murdered Edwin, and had he been detected compulsively brooding over the scene of his crime—as such maniacs were said to do? Or, alternatively, had his past criminal associations, whatever they had been during his incarceration, endowed him with unusual acuity in such matters, so that he had really perceived correctly the presence of fear and guilt somewhere in Hanwell Court?

These questions occupied Honeybath's thoughts during the rest of his walk to the Hanwell Arms, and as they were inherently baffling they naturally received no answer. The pub proved to be an unpretending one, and he had to make his needs known to a man in the public bar. The man was civil but unenthusiastic; declared he must consult some higher authority; and withdrew after serving Honeybath with the pint of bitter it had occurred to him to ask for by way of indicating his goodwill towards the establishment. Honeybath retired to a bench in a corner and took stock of his surroundings.

Two undersized men close to him were chucking darts at a board on the opposite wall. He gathered almost at once from what he could follow of their conversation that they were natives of the place and worked at some racing stables close at hand. The surrounding downs, he remembered, supported numerous concerns of that sort. It was therefore probable that a larger group of men—there seemed to be seven or eight of them—at the other end of the bar were stable lads too. But almost at once he doubted this. Although evidently from a similarly unassuming level of society, there was definitely something alien and urban about them. An unsympathetic observer would have declared that there was a hint of the flashy to them too, and an acute one would have remarked that, although otherwise homogeneous, they divided in point of footwear into two sharply contrasting groups. One group wore very shiny shoes with elongated and pointed toes; the other, thick-soled and stubby boots suggestive of some athletic pursuit the violence of which made an element of in-built protective steel a prudent device. This group of persons seemed not much in its element in its present rural surroundings. There was seldom a moment when one or another individual was not to be distinguished as glancing furtively or warily around him; sometimes—and this was disconcerting—two or three together would turn and look fixedly at Honeybath; at other times they would all disperse about the bar, unconcernedly whistling; and after this they would all come together again and converse in a huddle. Honeybath found himself hoping that these rather disagreeable men were not putting up at the Hanwell Arms. But this was improbable. The pub couldn't run to more than two or three bedrooms all told.

And now one of the men crossed the room and stood beside Honeybath, but without having any apparent interest in him. He whistled gently and tunelessly; broke off to offer one of the stable lads some technical remark on the game; resumed whistling; and then did address Honeybath in the most casual fashion.

'You live around here?' he asked.

'No, sir, I do not.'

'Visitor, like?'

'I have friends in the neighbourhood.' Honeybath judged this to be veracious after a fashion, and not unduly informative. 'At a place called Hanwell Court.'

'Belong to the Queen, does it?' The man thus gratuitously catechizing Honeybath seemed impressed.

'I have no reason to suppose it to be, or ever to have been, Crown property. It describes itself, if you must know, as affording luxury residential accommodation for retired gentlefolk.' Honeybath had remembered this phrase from the Hanwell Court brochure, and he hoped it might choke this intrusive person off. And his questioner (who suddenly struck him as bearing what might be called a faint vocational resemblance to Mr Brown) did seem a little to lose interest. He continued, nevertheless.

'Your friends like that?'

'I find no occasion to discuss them with you.'

'No offence.' The man uttered these words in a tone of gentle admonishment which somehow contrived to sound distinctly threatening. 'Looking for a friend of our own, we are. See? Anxious to make contact on account of what you might call auld lang syne. Been seen in a car, he has, round about these parts.'

'I think it most unlikely that I can help you.' Honeybath had become aware of a certain stir—almost of agitation—at the other end of the bar. This deplorable person's companions were disapproving of his behaviour. They even seemed to be whistling him back to heel. They all looked of undistinguished intelligence, but perhaps this one was thicker than the rest. And Honeybath now believed that he understood the situation. Horse racing, although a pursuit so extensively favoured in England by the more affluent of the propertied class, had attached to it, he knew, an underworld of touts, tipsters and (if the phrase were permissible) straight crooks. One used constantly to be hearing about 'race-course gangs', and if the phrase appeared to have dropped a little out of use the thing itself probably lingered on. The gangs, of course, went in for hideous feuds. One of their main activities was slashing one another with razors. And he had stumbled upon such a gang now. Their present activity must be connected with one or another of those training establishments dotted around the neighbourhood.

Having arrived at this reasonable estimate of his situation, Honeybath was about to take some appropriate evasive action when he became aware that the ruffian who had challenged him was taking evasive action himself. He had muttered something which might have been 'No offence', repeated this time on a purely conciliatory note, and he was now shambling back to his companions, who clearly regarded him as having taken a technically inadmissible step. And then they *all* faded away. In a matter of seconds, as it seemed, the public bar was empty.

The barman now returned, accompanied by a woman clearly of superior standing in the pub. She appeared as surprised as she was gratified that an inquiry about accommodation should be forthcoming from a person of Honeybath's speech and bearing. This was scarcely promising in point of what he was likely to find in the way of entertainment at the Hanwell Arms. But the room he was shown was decently clean, and he closed with it at once—further encouraged, indeed, by the sound he had heard from the inn yard of two rapidly departing cars. The gang—the auld lang syne gang, as it might be called—was pursuing the hunt for its friend elsewhere. No doubt he would be found in a ditch that night, appropriately 'worked over', as such people were said to express the matter.

This macabre thought a little distressed Honeybath as he presently ate some indifferent cheese and distastefully plastic bread by way of luncheon. He then walked back to Hanwell Court.

XV

THE ENTRANCE HALL of the mansion was a spacious area, lofty and with dark-panelled walls on which hung sundry mediocre portraits of unknown eighteenth-century notabilities—these last having presumably 'gone with the house' when it was first appropriated to its present communal purpose. Being, moreover, handsomely carpeted and liberally supplied with sofas and easy-chairs in crimson leather, it was sufficiently habitable to be referred to from time to time by inadequately cultivated inmates as the 'lounge'. One would not have expected it ever to become the scene of indecorous behaviour. But as Honeybath entered it indecorous behaviour was undoubtedly going on.

It was being occasioned by Ambrose Prout, who was reprehending Brigadier Luxmoore in the most violent terms for some act of omission or commission which Honeybath for some moments failed to pick up. Mr Brown was assisting at this discreditable episode—although at present only in the passive sense of standing by and taking note.

Honeybath would have been annoyed—although perhaps unreasonably—by Prout's thus promptly turning up even had his behaviour been irreproachable, since he had by now come to view with the deepest suspicion the integrity of this confounded picture-pedlar's dealings with his brother-in-law's affairs. And if it was true that he might quite properly have been sent down by a prostrated Melissa as a representative of the family (which Honeybath himself, after all, was not), it yet couldn't have been for the purpose of making a vulgar scene. Or at least it was to be hoped not.

And it at once turned out, indeed, that the matter at issue was one about which neither Melissa nor anybody else beyond the walls of Hanwell Court could know anything as yet. Within the last hour there had been a burglary perpetrated on the premises. Or if not a burglary (which implies intent to commit a felony) at least a breaking-in. It had happened in those comfortable apartments which Edwin Lightfoot had now quitted for good. The door admitting to them from the body of the house had been locked by the police, who presumably proposed some routine examination of them later for anything that might throw light on the dead man's circumstances or state of mind. A passing servant, however, had heard somebody give what she described as 'a kind of sudden laugh' within, and had reported this perplexing mild indecency to Brigadier Luxmoore. The solitary policeman remaining in the house had been summoned; the door had been unlocked; and nothing in any way untowards had at first appeared. The constable, however, examined the windows with care. Although the rooms were on the first floor, a couple of the windows gave directly upon the flat roof of what had once been a billiard-room, and one of them had been forced open in what the constable declared with authority to be an unskilful manner. But the perpetrator could have taken his time had he desired to do so, since the disposition of the adjacent walls was such that he would have been virtually secure against observation.

It was this perplexing incident that Prout was creating about—and with a vehemence and agitation than Honeybath judged unseemly in the circumstances. That some sort of sneak-thief had conceivably been prowling the dead man's property was almost as shocking in itself as that he should have been mysteriously and rashly prompted to audible laughter. But matters were not improved by making a vulgar row.

Brown now revealed himself as being almost as upset as Prout. Honeybath recalled that Brown—if Gaunt, the somewhat eccentric stiletto man, was to be believed—had provided the establishment with obscurely professional advice on protecting itself against such depredations. So perhaps it was just that Brown's vanity was affronted by the ease with which an intruder had broken in. Luxmoore—a thoroughly reasonable man, but one whose job probably required him to be constantly smoothing ruffled feelings of one sort or another on the part of his inmates—was inclined to play the episode down. Not so, it appeared, the constable, who was now on the telephone, summoning higher authority back to the scene. And the constable, of course, was right. Honeybath saw this clearly. Hard upon Edwin's still totally mysterious death, Edwin's rooms had been raided by a person unknown. The obvious inference was that he had been concerned to secure, and remove or destroy, documents or other material of an incriminating character bearing upon the fatality. But it didn't seem to be this that was in Prout's mind, or in Brown's either.

Honeybath realized, too, that this fresh mystery affected his own position. He had felt, a little vaguely, that it would be in order for him to have some access to Edwin's rooms himself, and that this would at least rationalize his impulse to stay around as an observing presence for a time. In this assumption he had perhaps been encouraged by the apparent disposition of Adamson, that high-ranking officer, to take an open-and-shut view of the case. But in face of this new development the police would at least have to suspend their persuasion that Edwin had died because he was a melancholic or a drunk. And as a consequence of this they would be much indisposed to have an amateur assistant poking around where he had no business to be.

So Honeybath now rather regretted having booked that room at the Hanwell Arms. On the other hand he was determined not to let Ambrose Prout remain in any sense in command of the field. For Prout, he told himself, was up to no good. On the contrary, he was (if the expression was possible) up to *bad*. Honeybath even had a glimmering sense of what that *bad* might be. And as his mind now turned that way, one of those striking ideas of his came to him. Prout's present fuss and indignation was a blind. *He and the man who had broken into Edwin's rooms were confederates, fellow-conspirators.* It was as simple as that.

Or, of course, as complicated. What would Adamson say if he came forward with so bizarre a notion? Or the urbane Luxmoore, for that matter? Or even the still invisible Dr Michaelis? Why had Michaelis visited Prout in London? *Was Michaelis a conspirator too?* And what about Brown, of whom it was a tenable theory that he owned some sort of criminal past? *Was Brown one as well?* And what about that gang in the pub? Faced with these thronging suspicions, Honeybath suddenly felt very much on his own.

He also felt that he wanted to see Michaelis at once. He wanted to have it out with the man—although he wasn't, indeed, altogether clear about what he meant by 'it' in this connection. The cardinal fact about the Medical Superintendent—at least in relation to Edwin—was that he had revealed himself as an out-and-out Philistine. Hadn't he talked of Edwin's efforts to regain command of his art as he might talk of some old woman who had to be encouraged in her basket-work by way of 'occupational therapy'? Such a man couldn't have been in any sympathetic relationship with an artist; he wouldn't know whether Edwin was painting well or ill; he couldn't care less, so long as the employment was having a composing effect upon one whom he quite gratuitously regarded as his patient. Still, it did seem as if he and Edwin had fairly regularly conversed over a considerable period of time. What he had to say about Edwin's being, or not being, suicidally inclined, or as having, or having not, given way to secret nocturnal drinking, ought at least to be listened to. In this persuasion Honeybath slipped away from Brigadier Luxmoore and the two men pestering him, and made his way to Michaelis's subterranean quarters.

He knocked on the door, appeared to hear a summons from the interior, and entered the room. Michaelis's back was turned to him, and he was peering into the gloom of a bookcase so excessively Gothic in inspiration that it looked less like a bookcase than a tomb. Michaelis turned round, recognized Honeybath, and jumped. People don't often really jump out of their skins. The image is extremely extravagant. But that seemed to be roughly what Michaelis's spasmodic movement aimed at. Had Honeybath been Adamson, and had there been ranked behind him a posse of policemen brandishing truncheons and manacles, the man could not have been more alarmed. Honeybath had been told by Brown that panic was abroad in Hanwell Court. Here, surely, it was.

'Ah, good afternoon, Mr Honeybath. Can I help you in any way?' Michaelis had endeavoured to pull himself together. But the question was so absurd (being, no doubt, the man's customary formula when visited by inmates in a professional way) that Honeybath was for a moment at a loss how to answer it.

'Good afternoon,' he said. 'I came down to Hanwell at once when I heard the news. I hope not intrusively. You may recall that I was one of Edwin Lightfoot's oldest friends.'

'No, not at all. That is to say, yes—yes indeed. Won't you sit down?' As he made this suggestion, reasonable in itself, Michaelis looked wildly round his handsomely furnished room, as if despairing of any possibility of finding a chair in it. 'A marvellous day,' he said idiotically. And this was really too much for Honeybath.

'Dr Michaelis,' he said severely, 'Lightfoot's sudden tragic death is a sad and shocking thing. But you appear to me, if I may say so, in an unduly perturbed condition.' (He had been about to say 'in a filthy funk', but remembered it was an expression he hadn't used since his prep-school days. The alternative he had adopted perhaps erred, on the contrary, on the formal side.)

'Yes, of course. I mean, no—not at all. That is to say, I am considerably upset. I feel, Mr Honeybath, that I have failed in proper vigilance. Lightfoot was at risk, undoubtedly at risk. It was my duty to keep an eye on the situation.'

'At risk? In what sense, may I ask, do you employ the expression? Do you suppose anybody to have been threatening him?'

'Oh, no—no, indeed not!' Michaelis had actually done the jumping trick again—this time in a sedentary position, since he had collapsed into a chair. 'I mean simply that Lightfoot, as an advanced neuropath, was likely to be subject to suicidal impulses. And death by water, indeed, was precisely what I ought to have been apprehensive of. A uterine fixation, Mr Honeybath. Had he shot or hanged himself it would have been altogether more surprising.' Michaelis showed a flicker of returning confidence as he gained this mushy professional ground. 'So that was it,' he said firmly. 'But very sad, of course. A talented man, without a doubt. I was myself a great admirer of his work. And he was much liked here—very much liked. I hope that, despite any theological difficulty, there may later be a quiet memorial service in our local parish church.'

'Confound your hopes, sir!' Honeybath was suddenly very angry. 'And I do not believe that Lightfoot took his own life. Nor do I believe the revolting suggestion that a condition of inebriety caused him simply to tumble into that woman's disgusting tank. I do believe that my friend was murdered. And I intend to get to the bottom of the mystery, and see justice done.' Honeybath paused, surprised by his own words. It was as if this conviction had bobbed up and crystallized only in the act of his giving utterance to it. 'I give you fair warning,' he added, and realized that these words were more extraordinary still.

They certainly had a powerful effect on the wretched Medical Superintendent. His momentary attempt at a confident air vanished; his jaw sagged in an unnatural fashion, as if he were a bad actor registering an extreme of dismay; he stared dumbly at Honeybath for some seconds before speaking.

'The police!' he then said hoarsely. 'Do they believe that?'

'They well may. I am not in their confidence. They will certainly investigate the affair in the most thorough-going way. Any appearance of their taking much for granted is probably a kind of routine deception, Dr Michaelis.'

'They haven't taken anybody away? Prout, for example?'

'Prout is still upstairs, making a nuisance of himself to Brigadier Luxmoore.' Honeybath had thought Michaelis's question exceedingly odd, but not exactly enlightening. 'And as it appears that I am making myself a nuisance to you, I will bid you good afternoon.'

And Honeybath left the room with a curt nod. Michaelis's condition perplexed him, and he judged the whole situation required thinking over if he wasn't himself to risk some false step. He resolved to return to the Hanwell Arms at once, and there devote the evening to sorting out his ideas. In the hall he ran into Prout, who was now alone. It was only a fleeting encounter, since Prout plainly had no desire to converse. Honeybath derived a curious impression from it, all the same. Prout's agitation had left him, and he certainly wasn't in anything like Michaelis's state of panic. He looked, in fact, as if he too was feeling the need—and the disposition—to think matters out. And Prout (Honeybath found himself reflecting as he walked down the drive), although an objectionable person, had to be credited with the virtue of pertinacity. If he had resolved upon some course of wrong-doing, he wouldn't too lightly be put off.

PART THREE

THE EARTHSHAKER FALLS

XVI

I T W A S A beauteous evening, calm and free. Or thus did
Charles Honeybath, who was fond of the English poets,
reflect as he left the house and set off down the drive. The
broad sun was sinking down in its tranquillity, and a hush
had fallen upon the feathered songsters of the grove. There
was a solemn stillness broken only by the distant sound of
Hondas and Suzukis on which weary ploughmen were
speeding homewards along unfrequented bypaths and minor
roads surrounding the estate. The effect of all this was
composing, and also more agreeable than the immediate
prospect of the Hanwell Arms. In that unassuming hostelry
there would be a considerable interval before Honeybath
could hope to dine. It might even be an interval enlivened
by the arrival of a further gang of desperadoes. The pub
was conceivably a well-known rendezvous of such persons,
and he had failed to observe in it the sort of inner sanctum
labelled 'Residents Only' to which such places occasionally
run.

Honeybath, who had formed the perhaps extravagant
notion that Hanwell Court itself had become a haunt of the
criminal classes, was anxious to avoid any further contact
with people of that kidney. He decided to procrastinate any
such possibility by taking an hour's stroll in the park and its
environs. Pausing only for a further brief inspection of
Poseidon the Earthshaker (who was casting a particularly
minatory shadow in the low raking light), he set off in a

direction hitherto unexplored. It led him to an area in which the boundary of the park appeared indefinite; he crossed a stile and found himself in rough pasture; crossed a second stile and was on a narrow path threading an untended coppice. Clumps of hazel alternated with crowded and stunted grey poplar saplings; there were forests of nettles and mare's tails head-high; on either hand the ground rose in broken undulations to a near horizon marked here and there by dead elms; it rose, too, more gently as Honeybath moved ahead. He saw that he was in a coombe descending from the downs to the vale on the edge of which Hanwell Court lay. It was, he told himself, good Boy Scout territory.

But the only human being presently to come into view was far from juvenile. Honeybath heard the clop-clop of an axe or hatchet, rounded a thicket, and was looking at a patriarchal figure seated on a log in a small clearing. He had a pile of hazel branches beside him, and was shaping them into gads. Honeybath (who had enjoyed the inestimable benefit of a country childhood) knew that the rural pursuit here exhibited was that of the thatcher.

It seemed reasonable to pass the time of day (or evening) with this industrious character, and Honeybath advanced so as to come within earshot. He was halted, however, and to an effect of considerable alarm, by a sudden and extra-ordinary manifestation at the farther side of the glade. On a fallen poplar there certain twigs had gently parted, and a gleaming metallic object had been protruded between them. There could be not the slightest doubt as to what the object was. It was the barrel of a rifle. And it was trained upon the aged rustic bowed unconsciously over his humble task.

Honeybath uttered a warning shout. It seemed the only thing to do. On the thatcher it had no effect; he simply went on clop-clopping. But the rifle vanished instantly; there was a sound of snapping twigs; a momentary glimpse of a human form, bent and running; and then the incident was as if it had never been.

Honeybath was much too horrified to be afraid. What hideous vendetta, what unspeakable act of bucolic vengeance, had his timely arrival on the scene providentially averted? He hurried forward and with urgent words implored the thatcher to seek safety in instant flight. In vain! The thatcher was gratified by his interest but indisposed to communication. He turned out, in fact, to be deaf and dumb.

What on earth was to be done? Simply to leave this unfortunate exposed to the danger of a second attack was a course of conduct quite unthinkable. It was true that the assailant had scarcely showed himself a determined adversary. The appearance, in the person of Honeybath, of an elderly man as defenceless as his proposed victim had scared him off—or had done so at least for a time. But was it not only too likely that he would continue to lurk around, and would renew his purpose as soon as Honeybath departed from the scene? There appeared to be no solution to this dilemma.

But fortunately it was not so. Honeybath's appearance had at least occasioned an interruption in this devoted peasant's labours. Honeybath's urgency, it may be, he had interpreted simply as a vigorous injunction to call it a day. The thatcher grinned, nodded, produced a large watch from a pocket, studied its findings with care—and then stood up, shouldered his axe, produced a gobbling sound plainly cordial in tone, and walked away. And by good luck he walked away in the direction diametrically opposite to that by which his would-be assassin had effected his retreat.

As for Honeybath, he turned back on his own own tracks and hoped for the best. If he were senselessly made away with by a total stranger, it couldn't be helped. He must simply try to get out of the coombe and gain the nearest habitation from which he could report the shocking incident he had witnessed to the police. And this for a time remained his sole preoccupation. It would be almost true to say that Hanwell Court and all its mystery had been incontinently banished from his head.

And soon, indeed, he had something new to worry about. He was being followed. Or rather, at one moment he was being followed, and at another (and incredibly quickly) he had been overtaken, slipped past, and made the object of an ambush threatening from the front. Or were there two of these people—or even a whole platoon of them? If so, they constituted some sort of uniformed guerrilla group. For several times he caught a glimpse of a human figure—usually the backside of a human figure on all fours or on its belly—identically habited. It is probable that all this didn't go on for as long as he imagined. And it came to an end quite suddenly. The man with the rifle (for there was only he) must have been at fault in some way, and had imagined Honeybath to be where he was not. And Honeybath (who confessedly was standing not upon the order of his going but going at once) simply stumbled over his prone form and came to the ground beside him. He scrambled to his feet, prepared to fight for his life, dimly feeling that to grab the rifle was his only chance of survival. His pursuer scrambled up too, and the two men faced one another. For Honeybath one glance was enough. The man's bearing, his mere attire, flashed the truth upon him. This was Colonel Dacre, decidedly strayed from his rifle range. And he himself had very nearly been Admiral Emery.

'One point down,' Colonel Dacre said. 'One can't always win.'

'I suppose not.' Honeybath found that extreme embarrassment had now taken the place of his alarm. For the colonel was quite clearly *not* a homicidal maniac. He was a merely ludicrous eccentric who had been enacting a grotesque juvenile fantasy. So the situation had become simply uncomfortable. To have come upon, to have been involved with such puerility was somehow demeaning in itself. It was as if—Honeybath thought—one had been obliged to watch 'performing' elephants or bears in a wretched little circus, or a respectable citizen reduced to infantile behaviour by a stage hypnotist. One wanted to walk out.

But this delicacy of feeling, although it was such as an artist might be expected to exhibit, Honeybath knew to be exaggerated and to demand control. His best course would be to take his cue from what Dacre had just said, and regard himself as having been joined in a very ordinary sort of game.

'Most interesting, sir,' he said. 'You must tell me about the rules. Perhaps while we retrace our steps through the coombe.' It would be only a reasonable precaution, he felt, to hasten back to the haunts of men. For his new interpretation of the affair might be at fault, after all.

'Love and war, sir,' the colonel said. 'No rules in either of them. And sharpshooters need initiative, vigilance, constant training if they are to come out on top.'

'Very true.' Honeybath, relieved to find Dacre falling peaceably into step beside him, accepted this mild rebuke. 'And you are in training yourself?'

'Precisely so. Of course I put in much time on my range. But one must constantly habituate oneself to the conditions of the field. The time is coming, you know! We may have to take to the woods for an indefinite period, but in the end we shall win the day. And the sharpshooters will be crucial. It was a French sharpshooter who got Nelson, you know— and that was almost a decisive thing. And Wellington in the Peninsula found that he had to train sharpshooters to match the enemy's. "Learn to drop your man, and be damned," he said. A good motto for the troops.'

'An admirable one, I am sure.' Honeybath found that it was possible to receive these fragments of military and naval history with decent respect. Colonel Dacre was a kind of Boy Scout after all. He was resolved to Be Prepared.

'May I introduce myself? My name is Rupert Dacre, and I live at Hanwell Court. May I inquire whether you have recently come to live there yourself? If so, I apologize for not having made your acquaintance earlier.'

'My name is Charles Honeybath, and I am a painter.' Honeybath found this shift to polite exchanges comforting. 'The palette and not the sword, Colonel Dacre, is what I live by. I had thought of coming to Hanwell for a time, but changed my plans. I had a close friend there, Edwin Lightfoot, about whose sad death you will have heard.'

'Yes, indeed. I am very, very sorry. I condole with you on the loss of your friend. A delightful man. And now they are talking scandal about him. He drowned because he was drunk. Or he made away with himself. Twaddle—and twaddle of a disgusting sort. He was plainly the victim of foul play. I much wish that I had been able to stand guard over him. Or had merely been within a couple of hundred yards. I could have picked his assailant off, you know. Yes, picked him off.'

'I am sure you could.' Honeybath was warming to Colonel Dacre. It looked as if he had found an ally in him. 'And for my own part, I am determined to get at the truth.'

'Capital! I am delighted to hear you say so, Mr Honeybath. Are you returning to the house now?'

'No—I am putting up for the night at the inn.'

'Then let me accompany you so far. It will afford me opportunity to thank you more adequately for having joined in the exercise.'

Although this was perhaps an odd way of describing Honeybath's recent experience, it could reasonably be received as an *amende honorable* agreeably consonant with Colonel Dacre's military character. And the colonel followed it up as they walked with some courteous expressions of his regard for Edwin.

'I think I may claim,' he said, 'to have got to know him fairly well. I liked his imaginative side.'

'He certainly possessed that.'

'He had a fancy at times for being somebody else. It sounds peculiar, but I found it attractive. We would go out together, and he would become a Red Indian. A Cherokee, say, or a Cheyenne.'

'Edwin would be quite good at that.'

'Yes, indeed. And he would challenge me to track him down. That sort of thing. It could be quite instructive. But chiefly, of course, I admired him as a painter. Do you know that he made some amusing portrait-sketches at Hanwell?'

'Yes, I do.'

'Powerful caricatures, some of them. I recall one in particular, a group of several of us round a card table, which reminded me of Leonardo's *Five Grotesque Heads* in the Royal Library at Windsor. No doubt you recall that small masterpiece.'

'I certainly do.' Honeybath had to restrain himself from glancing at Colonel Dacre in some astonishment.

'But I was very glad that Lightfoot continued his serious painting. He was rather reticent about it. But I saw one of his more recent paintings just after he had completed it. It brought back to me much of his earlier work as I remember it. *A Visionary Townscape* was the title I gave it in my own mind. Quite equal to Kokoschka. Magnificent.'

'I'd like to see that.' Honeybath was so surprised by this revelation of a quite unsuspected side to the sharpshooter of

Hanwell Court that for some moments he said no more.
The quality of Dacre's taste and judgement remained an
unknown quantity, but it was clear that he was not un-
informed in artistic matters. A question occurred to him.
'Was Lightfoot pleased with it?' he asked.

'Curiously enough, I would say that he was not. But then
he was not, I fear, in general a happy man. Am I right, Mr
Honeybath?'

'Quite right.'

'I sometimes suspected him of feeling that his career had
in some way gone wrong; that he had failed to fulfil himself. It is something that we all in one degree or another
are liable to, would you not say? But here, I see, is your
inn, and I must take my leave of you.'

Honeybath entered the Hanwell Arms without the need
to look out for desperadoes so much as occurring to him.
Colonel Dacre had given him something quite different to
think about. But just what that something was he didn't
yet see.

XVII

HALF AN HOUR later, and in quest of an *apéritif* the
digestive virtues of which might soon be urgently called
upon in face of the Hanwell Arm's cuisine, Honeybath went
into the bar. This time, there were no gangsters present.
There was, however, Melissa—a circumstance almost
equally disconcerting. Melissa had, of course, every right to
be in the vicinity; indeed, it would have been unbecoming
were she not. To have remained undisturbed in whatever
sort of Deep Meditation she was at present going in for
would have been, so to speak, too meditative by far. But it
was tiresome of her—Honeybath most unreasonably thought
—to have found her way to this pub. How was he to think
matters out with the confounded woman latching on to him?
And she would certainly do that. She was the latching-on
sort.

But these were uncharitable sentiments to harbour about
a woman so recently bereaved, and Honeybath repressed
them. Melissa was standing at the bar, narrowly monitoring
the barman as he mixed her some approximation to a
martini. It was only when she had assured herself there had
been no short measure that she evinced any knowledge of
Honeybath's presence.

'My dear Melissa, this is a very sad occasion, and I
condole with you deeply.' It had been quite properly,
Honeybath judged, that he had thus been left to speak first.
And Melissa looked a good deal stricken; although separated

and estranged from her husband for what was now a considerable period of time, she had presumably by no means lost all feeling for him.

'I suppose I should be grateful to him,' Melissa said—to the surprise of the barman, who imagined himself to be addressed. 'But he started it all, didn't he? Egging him on to go and live in that horrible place.'

'Melissa, come and sit down.' As often before, Honeybath felt that intelligible conversation with poor Edwin's wife simply could not be conducted standing at a bar or anywhere else. So he took her by the arm, led her firmly over to a settee, and by way of letting her compose herself returned to the bar and ordered his own drink. 'I know they have had to take Edwin's body away,' he said when he had himself sat down. 'There always has to be an examination by doctors after a sudden and unattended death. But I am sure it will be possible to make normal funeral arrangements quite soon. Have you seen anybody at the house yet?'

'What do you mean, Charles, by an unattended death? *Somebody* was there. We can be quite sure of that.'

'Well, yes.' Honeybath took a moment to see that Melissa's last remark at least revealed a point of view close to his own. 'I meant merely a death where there has been no medical attendance immediately beforehand.'

'They have that doctor up there. The one I didn't care for, and who got thick with Ambrose.'

'Ah, Dr Michaelis. Well, there is no suggestion that he was treating Edwin in any way. Or not since his return from abroad. By the way, Melissa, were you and Edwin writing to one another?'

'It would be no business of yours if we were. But as a matter of fact we were not.' Melissa was getting rapidly through her martini—probably in the interest of being treated to another. 'What do you want to know for?'

'Because he might have said something about his painting. I was talking earlier this evening to a man—quite a knowledgeable man—who believes himself to have seen a distinctly good recent picture. Edwin, it seems, showed it to him. But my own impression is that nothing was coming back to Edwin of anything like his old power. It's puzzling.'

'It's nothing of the kind. It was just something out of Edwin's secret store of the things from the old days. And the man you were talking to got a muddled idea that it was new. I'm convinced those pictures exist, you know. But what *I* don't know is how much Ambrose knows about it.' Melissa drained her glass and pushed it across the table towards Honeybath. He picked it up willingly enough. This act of necessary replenishment was going to give him a few moments in which to think. That there really was some mystery about Edwin's painting was now clear to him; and it looked as if he and Melissa were again on the same wavelength in the matter. But that the situation as he dimly saw it bore any relationship to the manner of Edwin's death seemed totally incredible. For the moment, he thought as he returned with the second martini, he'd change the subject, or at least approach it from another direction.

'Why are you putting up at this pub, Melissa?' he asked. 'It doesn't look at all promising to me. Surely they'd have thought it proper to find you a room at Hanwell Court.'

'They probably did. I saw a man called Luxmoore. A gentleman—which is more than can be said for your Dr What's-his-name. He wanted to hand me over to his wife. But I wasn't going to spend a night under the same roof as *her*.'

'As Mrs Luxmoore? My dear Melissa, you can't know anything about her.'

'Not Mrs Luxmoore, Charles. That woman. The murderess.'

'*The murderess*? In heaven's name . . .'

'Lady Thingummy. You know how Edwin exhibited a funny picture of her. It wasn't a very decent thing to do, I daresay. He didn't deserve to be murdered for it, all the same. But Lady Thingummy . . .'

'Lady Munden.'

'Lady Munden is mad, of course. They're *all* mad at Hanwell Court. You shoved Edwin into a bloody bin, Charles. Morally, you are the murderer yourself.'

'My dear Melissa!' It came to Honeybath with a shock of horror that there was perhaps some atom of truth in this macabre suggestion. He had undeniably landed Edwin among a funny crowd from which he had himself shied away. 'Never mind about it morally,' he said. 'Just consider the matter practically. How on earth could Lady Munden, even if feeling like Lady Macbeth, have managed to murder Edwin?'

'By setting a booby-trap, of course, in her horrible pool. Filling it with things like Deadly Nightshade, only of a watery sort. Then she took him for a quiet evening walk— probably on the strength of the most disgusting and shameful enticements—and simply tipped him in. Stuff like that can sting, can't it, just like jellyfishes? Poor Edwin died instantly.'

'In that case, the post-mortem would reveal . . .'

'It won't reveal anything. She'd make sure that the stuff is unknown to science. Hell hath no fury like a woman scorned.'

At this point of extreme irrationality on Melissa's part Honeybath was made aware of the barman as making covert beckoning signs to him. He picked up his own empty glass and went over to the man. Melissa, he thought, was quite as mad as any of the residents at Hanwell Court admitted on Michaelis's quota system. And it was clear that he had to spend the rest of the evening with her. It was a disheartening thought. He put down his glass with a gesture indicating that it should be filled again.

'Well,' he demanded brusquely, 'what is it?'

'All arranged, sir.' The barman spoke in a hoarse whisper. 'The missus has arranged it. In the next room, the lady will be. And there's a nice quiet communicating door.'

'My good man . . .' Outraged, Honeybath was at a loss for further words.

'And no reason for your not having your dinner at the same table, sir. Very quiet we are just now—very quiet indeed. And nobody answers questions here if any of them private 'tecs come. Discreet, we are—and just hope you'll remember us kindly.'

This shocking relevation of the *mores* and assumptions of the Hanwell Arms was almost too much for Honeybath, who was a man of unimpaired probity in matters of sexual conduct. In addition to which he couldn't conceive himself as wanting under any circumstances whatever to get into bed with Melissa. He had a strong impulse to bolt from the place and vanish into the night. But he managed to control himself.

'You are under a vulgar misapprehension,' he said with grim dignity. 'The lady and I are very old friends. And her husband, as it happens, died this morning.'

He picked up his drink and returned to Melissa. The ideas in *her* head were as dotty as those in the barman's, although of a different character. He was most unlikely to get a single sensible thought out of her about the horrible business in which they were both involved. But for the rest of their encounter he would be as kind to her, as patiently tolerant, as he could possibly be.

XVIII

THE VIRTUOUS RESOLUTION just recorded
turned out to involve keeping Honeybath from his bed until
midnight. Melissa had a great deal on which to unburden
herself—and most of it concerned the criminality of Lady
Munden and the means that must be taken to unmask her.
Honeybath didn't for a moment believe that Lady Munden
had carried out a cold-blooded murdering of Edwin. It
might just be possible to conceive that, enraged by the
memory of the insult that had been offered her on the walls
of Burlington House, she could have picked up a paper-
weight or a candlestick and brained its perpetrator forth-
with. But that she had prepared the macabre booby-trap of
Melissa's imagining was entirely beyond credence. It seemed
to Honeybath that some curious guilt-mechanism was
operative in Edwin's widow. She had to have a woman in
the picture upon whom she could unload, as it were, the
ditching of Edwin—and this in a quite literal sense.

It would normally have given Honeybath considerable
satisfaction to achieve a psychological insight of this order.
But now a curious thing was happening to him. Although
resolved to solve the mystery of Edwin's death, he was really
more concerned about the mystery of Edwin's pictures. Just
what had been going on? That *something* had been going
on, he was now convinced. He even suspected that it was
something which, if not cleared up, might somehow impair
Edwin's posthumous reputation. And to safeguard that was

even more important than to bring Edwin's killer to justice.

He got no further with this thought until he was in bed, and it then occupied his mind for some hours before he got off to sleep. What, for a start, did he know with tolerable certainty? It seemed necessary to believe that certain hitherto unknown early Lightfoots did exist. But that there was a whole bunch of them that had never been sold or even exhibited was highly improbable. Indeed, something like certainty came in here too. Though he could have given no precise year by year account of Edwin's output during his great period, he did have a clear sense of what might be called its tempo. He knew Edwin's working habits then, and the extent of the periods during which, like any other artist, he had to let his full creative power take time off. Half a dozen fully achieved major pictures might possibly exist unknown to Honeybath himself. More than that would require the positing of a secretiveness and evasiveness on Edwin's part which would surely be foreign even to so quirky and freakish a character as he had frequently exhibited. Even so, half a dozen such pictures, if brought together and put on show for the first time, would create a sensation in the art world and undoubtedly be worth a great deal of money. So suppose some of them had been in the possession of Edwin himself, and without anyone else being aware of their existence. A thief who got hold of them could put up any story he pleased about how they had come to be his lawful property. And nobody could contradict him. *Or nobody except Edwin himself.*

Turning over restlessly in a bed that audibly protested against his slightest movement, Honeybath faced this grim thought. He also faced the disturbing image of Ambrose Prout and the dubious name of Mrs Gutermann-Seuss of Brighton. It must be supposed that the lady really existed, since Prout could not be so foolish as simply to make her up.

But wasn't there something suspicious, a kind of faking of verisimilar detail, in the story of this person's first producing a forged Lightfoot and later an authentic one? Had Prout simply stolen the little batch of pictures, either piecemeal or at one fell swoop, and then selected Mrs Gutermann-Seuss to fabricate a title to them? Had he done this from a rash persuasion that poor Edwin was sufficiently gaga not to become aware of his loss—and had this proved not to be the case, with fatal consequences?

But then there was the testimony of Colonel Dacre, that unexpected connoisseur of the fine arts. He had been shown, and had greatly admired, a picture which Edwin had described to him as recent work. But this, unless Edwin had in some totally abnormal way intermittently recovered his former power, must have resulted from a rather pathetic and wholly innocent impulse of deception on Edwin's part. The incident afforded strong evidence that unknown pictures did exist; that they had been in Edwin's possession; and— an important point—that Edwin had been by no means forgetful and unconcerned about them.

There was the chronological aspect of all this to consider. Although he had failed to question Dacre closely on the point, it was Honeybath's impression that the incident to which he had referred was of comparatively recent date; that it had taken place, in fact, shortly before he and Edwin had departed for Italy. Edwin had then been in a state of considerable distress—that, indeed, had been the reason for their pilgrimage; and the fact added to the curiosity of his having been prompted at least not to correct a misconception as to the dating of the picture. But what about the whole hypothesis that unknown early Lightfoots existed? It had lodged itself in Ambrose Prout's mind a long time back: Honeybath couldn't recall quite when. The first definite date had been that of Prout's abortive visit to Brighton;

then there had been his letter received in Rome to the effect that with Mrs Gutermann-Seuss he had struck lucky after all, and hinting that there might be, so to speak, more treasure-trove in the pipe-line in that quarter. And it had been in Rome that Melissa had announced that this expectation had been fulfilled, and that her brother now possessed three early Lightfoots all told. This, of course, might have been untrue. Honeybath had the impression that there were plenty of lies blowing around.

Among the manufacturers of these he was inclined—but on grounds that remained obstinately indefinite—to accord Michaelis an honoured place. But if the Medical Superintendent was indeed implicated in some conspiracy, it could only be, surely, because Hanwell Court was the place—or at least had been the place—where those precious canvases were located. And from this, if it were so, there would follow the fairly secure inference that the Brighton lady was either implicated in the conspiracy or had in some way been made an innocent dupe. Mrs Gutermann-Seuss ought to be investigated. Honeybath fell asleep resolving to seek her out.

It was a resolve still with him when he woke up next morning. So was the conviction that, for the present at least, he wanted to have nothing more to do with Hanwell Court. Melissa's arrival on the scene appeared to be the controlling factor here. It was a little odd, since she was pretty well the only person around whom he continued to judge incapable of harbouring one dark design or another. But Melissa had decidedly said nothing to suggest that she welcomed his having turned up in any way, and it could be only in an awkwardly intrusive role that he continued on the scene. He rose early, scribbled a note to be handed to her, and contrived to secure a conveyance to take him to the railway station. He was in Brighton by lunch-time and provided with a room for the night—but this time in a reassuringly solid hotel understood to have been extensively frequented by the nobility of a former time. Brighton had later become, of course, something of a gangsters' haunt—at least if one were to accept the testimony of Mr Graham Greene. But nothing of the kind was in evidence. Honeybath looked back on the Hanwell Arms without regret.

The telephone directory made manifest the fact that Mrs Gutermann-Seuss, at least, was the figment of nobody's imagination, and a preliminary reconnaissance established her abode as an enormous mansion occupying an elevated situation on the Marine Parade. Had it not presented, as it decidedly did, a somewhat run-down appearance, the inescapable inference would have been that its proprietor was in the enjoyment of affluence. Honeybath took a turn along the front to think things over, and then returned and rang the bell. The bell failed to function, so he knocked on the door. After a pause he banged very loudly, and this not wholly civil behaviour yielded results. There was a slithering sound as of ill-fitting slippers on a tiled floor, the door opened, and there was revealed an elderly woman who appeared to be having trouble with her hair. Although it was mid-afternoon, she was dressed in what Honeybath thought of as a kimono, so that it was to be feared that he had disturbed her during a period of repose.

'Good afternoon,' Honeybath said politely. 'Mrs Gutermann-Seuss?'

'Nothing today, thank you.' The woman said this vaguely and quite inoffensively.

'I must apologize for disturbing you. My name is Honeybath . . .'

'I never encourage beggars.' This also came without animus, but so promptly that Honeybath's name might have been taken instantly to reveal him as some mendicant notorious along the whole south coast of England.

'. . . and I have called,' Honeybath continued rather desperately, 'to inquire about certain pictures.'

'Pictures?' The expression of Mrs Gutermann-Seuss was quite blank, as if the class of objects thus denominated were wholly unknown to her. 'Would you care to come in?' she asked unexpectedly, and stood back from the door. As she did so a shrill whistle made itself heard somewhere in the depths of the house : momentarily low, and then rising to a pitch as of desertion and despair. 'The kettle,' Mrs Gutermann-Suess said. 'You'll have to wait.' And she disappeared first into half-light and then into a near-darkness in which her entire establishment seemed to repose.

Honeybath found himself in a large hall. It was hung with pictures frame to frame and reaching to the ceiling; most of the floor-space was invisible beneath huddled furniture and piled bric-a-brac over which spiders had spun their webs for many a year. A handsome staircase, however, was comparatively unencumbered, and was hung with a rising tier of photographs, all the portraits of male persons, and all inscribed with greetings and signatures in the manner particularly favoured by the theatrical classes. These, however, were not actors, and Honeybath advanced and inspected them cautiously. *Cordially, Andrew Mellon*, he read. *Yours, Samuel H. Cress . . . H. H. Huntington, California . . . Frick . . . Adam Verver, American City . . . With kind regards, B. Berenson . . . Gratefully, Joseph Duveen.* Everybody who had ever bought anything (or flogged anything) in a sufficiently big way was here. There could be no doubt of the standing at least of the original Mr Gutermann-Seuss. But who was the lady who now bore his name?

She proved to be his grandson's widow—and stranded amid all these proliferations of abandoned art (the bad buys and failed baits, one had to suppose) to her own complete bewilderment. There could never have been woman more totally without instinct for or interest in the deliverances of art than the present Mrs Gutermann-Seuss. She gave Honeybath tea (that was what the kettle had been for) and was perfectly willing to talk.

'Do you know a man called Ambrose Prout?' Honeybath asked baldly.

'Mr Prout? Oh, yes. He comes and goes.'

'On business?'

'He takes one thing or another. And leaves this or that.'

'*Leaves* this or that?'

'He buys pictures or not pictures but perhaps something else of one sort or another sort. In Brighton or perhaps not in Brighton but round about. And stores them with me for a time. Just tucks them away in one corner or another. On top of this or under that, perhaps.'

'And does he buy things from you too?'

'Oh, yes. Pictures, mostly. There are a great many, you know. Some in one room and some in another. And in the cellars.'

'I see. May I ask if he pays you in cash, Mrs Gutermann-Seuss?'

'Yes. He seems to like cash. I quite like it too. It's handy in one way and another.'

'Do you sign receipts for him?'

'Receipts?' It appeared to be with difficulty that Mrs Gutermann-Seuss identified the nature of these instruments in her mind. 'Yes, receipts. Or things like that. I don't much look at them, I suppose. There's nothing of any importance left in this house, you see. I was told that, or something like that, years and years ago. But it's quite comfortable. They say the roof leaks. But that's four floors up—or is it five? I don't go to look, so it doesn't bother me. Will you have

another cup of tea? Or a rock bun? I haven't brought the
rock buns. But I think I have some put away somewhere.'

Honeybath declined rock buns but accepted a second cup
of tea, which at least gave him time to look around him.
But the notion of conducting any search of the place was
wholly out of the question. If Prout had tucked away another
early Lightfoot or two amid this vast jungle of junk he alone
could find them again. Short of an army of qualified persons,
the situation was just that. In fact Prout's discovery of Mrs
Gutermann-Seuss was an astounding instance of serendipity.
And his exploitation of it amounted to genius. Honeybath
presently took his leave (Mrs Gutermann-Seuss having
proved completely incurious about the object of his visit),
and retired to the comforts of his hotel. He had at least exchanged doubt for certainty in the matters of nefarious
activity on the part of poor Edwin's brother-in-law.

Over his *apéritif* that evening—this time reassuringly consumed among persons of the polite or quasi-polite class—a
useful, if fragmentary, perception came to him. What had
been the immediate occasion of Edwin's suddenly breaking
off their Italian holiday and insisting on returning to
England? Considering this question earlier, he had taken the
reason to have been simply the general upsettingness of
Melissa's turning up on them in that restaurant in Rome.
But now he recalled that Edwin had said something very
explicit as the taxi took them back to their hotel. He was
going back to Hanwell Court, he had declared, in order 'to
clear things up there'. And he certainly hadn't employed
this phrase in the sense of 'to tidy up'—perhaps before
quitting the place. He had been envisaging something much
more significant than that. He had been intending to
elucidate something. Just what, Honeybath now had to
elucidate himself. So what had occurred at that meeting
with Melissa that could have set Edwin's mind in this

direction? Suddenly Honeybath knew the answer. It had been Melissa's announcement that Prout was now claiming to possess no less than three of those hypothetical lost early Lightfoots. That, somehow, had been too much for Edwin. It was this situation that he had said he was going to clear up. And it had been at Hanwell Court that he proposed to do it. He had returned there. And within a very short space of days he was dead.

All in all—Honeybath told himself with a strange mingling of satisfaction, horror and dismay—things were looking bad for Ambrose Prout.

XIX

HE PAID A call on Prout. It was perhaps an odd way of distinguishing one whom he was beginning seriously to suspect of homicide, and at first he had favoured the alternative plan of going to see the exalted Adamson at the London Metropolitan Police Office instead. Honeybath knew enough about the organization of the constabulary in the British Isles to be aware that a certain improbability had attended the prompt turning up of such a person in the wilds of Berkshire so hard upon Edwin's death. Adamson was almost part of the mystery—which was something dead against the canons of the *roman policier* affair now thickening around Charles Honeybath R.A. And as Adamson certainly couldn't be said to have taken Honeybath into his confidence, Honeybath hesitated, perhaps somewhat irrationally, before making any corresponding movement himself.

Quite aside from this, moreover, it was only fair that Edwin's brother-in-law should be taxed (or at least tested) in a private manner before being denounced to the police. Honeybath felt this to be the civilized thing, even if the situation were to turn into an unusual one. After breakfast—he resolved as he prepared that simple meal for himself—he would go straight to Prout's flat. If he arrived early enough, he would almost certainly find its owner in.

There can be no doubt that he was also hoping to find something else as well. The problem of Edwin's lost paintings was still predominating in his mind even over the problem of Edwin's death. Nothing could really be *done* about Edwin's death, apart from giving Nemesis a nudge and setting her to work. He knew that ultimately there was going to be no more than a flawed satisfaction obtainable from that. He suspected that it would be more flawed under the present law of the land. It must have been very shocking to have been responsible for having a man hanged. But being aware of having sent to prison a man who was still there after twenty years would conceivably be worse.

About the pictures something *could* be done. If they existed (as he now believed them to do) they could be recovered from fraudulent hands, specious representations, perhaps clandestine or semi-clandestine sale. That would be a real service to Edwin's memory.

More simply, Honeybath just longed to see more of Edwin's work from the grand time. And it seemed probable that, if he was forceful enough, he could compel Prout to produce it. He didn't now think out a plan of campaign in any detail. He would act as the spirit prompted when the moment came. Only he wouldn't come away baffled. There had been quite enough of bafflement already in this affair.

Prout was a bachelor, and answered his own bell. He said, 'Ah, Charles—good morning!' in a commonplace way before immediately standing back to let Honeybath enter. He was wary but couldn't have been called nervous. If he and Dr Michaelis were partners in crime, then it was he who would prove the tough one. He owned, for one thing, a dogged acquisitiveness, an immense cupidity. If he had possessed himself of certain objects worth a great deal of money, he would hold on to them with a grip as strong as a badger's jaw.

'I've seen Mrs Gutermann-Seuss,' Honeybath said.

'Capital! Do sit down, my dear Charles.' Prout had perhaps drawn a long breath. 'Can I make you some coffee?'

'Thank you, no. She seems a very simple woman.'

'She's certainly not a very effective one. It was the first Gutermann-Seuss who was the swell, you know. Quite at the top of his tree. Do you know Verver's *The Spoils of Darius*? A wonderfully revealing account of collector's mania in the great age. And there's an amusing account of Verver's making a trip to Brighton to relieve Gutermann-Seuss the First of some Oriental tiles. Gutermann-Seuss the Second carried on successfully for a time—as his having done a little business with poor Edwin shows. But he took to drink and the business began to go to pot. Gutermann-Seuss the Third was wholly incompetent even when dead sober. His widow may be described as quite bright in comparison with him. Disreputable dealers—pure jackals—moved in, and cleared out for a song anything worth taking. Or so they thought. But they missed those Lightfoots.'

'And you did not. You bought them? Or did you just offer to take them away?'

'Of course I bought them—and for quite respectable sums. Would you care to see the receipts?'

'No. But I'd like to see the pictures themselves, please.'

'Ah.'

Honeybath waited. The monosyllable, he thought, had betrayed indecision. He rather expected Prout to say something like, 'They've all gone to be cleaned'. But this didn't happen.

'You can see the zinnias,' he said briefly. 'It's the only one here. Come this way.'

Honeybath followed Prout into another room. And there the picture was. It was quite small, a bunch of flowers in a Chinese pot. It stood perched against a pile of books on a table, and in rather a poor light. But there could be no doubt about it—none whatever. Honeybath was very much moved. He didn't fail, however, to go close up to it at once and peer at the bottom left-hand corner. As always with Edwin, it was signed and meticulously dated. The date was right too.

Honeybath stood back a little, and took his time. It was an important moment. It would be fair to say, after all, that he probably had a surer instinct for Edwin's work than anybody else in the world. He wasn't looking at a forgery.

'Very pretty,' he said. 'Are the others all as small as this? You could carry it away in a brief-case.'

'Lord, no! You can call this the mere *hors d'oeuvre*, my dear Charles. The others are major compositions. You'll see them one day.'

'No doubt.' Honeybath judged that there had been a faint impudence in this last throw-away remark. 'There were major pictures by Edwin Lightfoot tucked out of sight among all the junk in that Brighton house? And you nosed them out?'

'Just that. I was tremendously excited, as you can guess. Never such a moment there since the good Adam Verver of American City found his doubtless priceless tiles. It's almost time for a drink.'

'It's nothing of the sort.' Honeybath looked at the picture again, vaguely troubled. Had he ever seen it before? The mere history of his close relationship with Edwin suggested that this was possible. But could he have forgotten it? This was *not* possible—or so he told himself. Yet his memory had faintly stirred. 'We'll go back to your other room,' he said abruptly, and turned away.

It was Honeybath who had a moment of indecision now. As well as having no doubt about the zinnias, he had no doubt about Mrs Gutermann-Seuss either. Neither this picture nor the others had ever reposed amid the forlorn detritus of the arts over which she unregardingly presided in that dismal Brighton house. She could be forgotten about, or forgotten about unless and until some legal row blew up about the just proprietorship of the rediscovered pictures. When that happened it might all be mixed up with a sensational murder trial. And the grim business of Edwin's death was now the next item on the carpet with Edwin's scoundrelly brother-in-law.

But ought it to be? Honeybath was certain that he owned no impulse to funk a confrontation, even if it ended with Prout taking a swipe at his skull with a poker. But Prout, he had decided, was tough. A nut, in fact, harder to crack than most craniums would be. It was Michaelis who might be said to represent the soft underbelly of the mystery. Before Prout was alerted to any imminent danger, it would be good tactics to have a go at the Medical Superintendent at Hanwell Court.

That there was danger not far off, both men must surely know. It was likely that there existed constant communication between them. They could not possibly be in any doubt that, once the hanky-panky over the lost pictures was suspected and came under investigation, they would themselves be in the front line of suspects in the mind of anybody who believed Edwin's death to have been a matter of foul play. So had they a strong sense, Honeybath wondered, that the tide was turning against them? Were they in constant fear that, in one way or another, they might slip up?

And there was another question about the pair. Had they planned Edwin's death from the start? Looked at one way, their whole project could be thought to have required it. They were proposing to steal, and Prout was proposing to assert his legal ownership of, a number of paintings which Edwin had, for reasons hidden in the depth of his own strange personality, concealed and presumably cherished. How could they hope simply to make off with them without his becoming so much as aware of the fact?

There was an answer to this. Michaelis had the cock-sureness about the inside of other people's heads that was a kind of professional risk with persons of his kidney. Prout had for long harboured the notion that Edwin's mind, and particularly his memory, were quite extravagantly in decay. Together they might have decided that they could so work things that their depredations might never transpire. Indeed, the simple psychological likelihood lay here. There was something excessive and unverisimilar in the notion of amateur sneak-thieves planning deliberate murder from the start. They had killed Edwin as an emergency measure when he turned out to be much more alert than they had supposed. It was fatally that he had returned to Hanwell Court instantly upon the report that Prout had come into the possession of three early Lightfoots. Rapidly altering and augmenting their design, the thieves had promptly made away with him.

It was a situation more hazardous than they had bargained for. But although both were equally involved, it had been only Michaelis who had been thrown into patent panic. Yes, Michaelis was the weak spot. Michaelis was the man to go for now. Having come rapidly to this conclusion, Honeybath resolved to pick up a taxi the moment he quitted Prout's flat, drive straight to Paddington, and make for Hanwell by the first available train. Prout would probably take a little time to ponder the significance of Honeybath's visit before taking any action. It might even be possible to corner Michaelis before any contact between the conspirators had been made.

'I'm delighted to have seen the zinnias,' he said pacifically, 'and I look forward to seeing the others. But they are no substitute—are they?—for Edwin himself, poor fellow.' Honeybath felt bad as he thus endeavoured to administer a kind of Machiavellian bromide to the doubtless suspicious

Prout. 'Incidentally, Ambrose, what is your own idea about the manner of Edwin's death? From time to time, you know, I really have a suspicion that foul play was involved. But it scarcely seems a rational notion—for what enemies could a man like Edwin have? I'd like your opinion. Was it plain misadventure, would you say—just a matter of a false step in the dark?'

'It seems far the likeliest explanation.' Prout paused—decidedly wary now. 'Yet I sometimes doubt it too. Edwin, after all, had that thing about women. He had fits when he couldn't resist them. You remember how he even had in tarts when he was living alone in Holland Park.'

'Yes, I do remember that,' Honeybath said—and wondered whether he had lured Prout into some rather stupid double bluff. 'But I think that may just have been a matter of his feeling lonely, and having in a girl from the street to chat to. Scarcely a matter of a sexual urge at all. It does often happen, I believe.'

'No doubt. But don't forget, Charles, that it was a very rum place you landed him in.'

'Hanwell?'

'Yes, Hanwell. Half of the people clear nutters, including plenty of idle women. It wouldn't surprise me to learn that Edwin had got tangled up with two or three of them, and that some crazy fit of jealousy did the rest.'

'I see.' Honeybath offered this thoughtfully and judiciously, although he thought it even more absurd than Melissa's daft notion about Lady Munden. 'We must leave it all to the police,' he added vaguely, and got up to take his leave.

There was a taxi at the corner of the road. He hailed it, said 'Paddington!' to the driver, and jumped in. He doubted whether Prout had been deceived. But at least he was himself now vigorously on the move.

XX

IN THE TRAIN a disconcerting reflection came to our investigator. When that letter had arrived in Rome from Prout announcing the discovery of Edwin's zinnias Edwin had declared roundly that he had no memory of the thing, and had doubted whether he would recognize a zinnia if he saw it. But was this possible if the flower piece had been among those few undeclared canvasses that he had secretly cherished—or at least hidden away? Surely he must have taken a glance at them from time to time? It was hard not to suppose that his disavowal had been disingenuous; that he had quite pointlessly prevaricated. And this was unlike Edwin. He could be perverse and elusive, and he could happily spin you what were patent fantasies. But he didn't tell lies. Brooding on this small explicability, Honeybath felt rather hurt in his mind.

It was a sultry day, and had followed a sequence of sultry days. As soon as he had got out of London (where there is never anything to speak of that can be called weather in the common sense) Honeybath was aware of approaching storm, of thunder in the air. He was even a little nervous about it, since he was setting out on this unpremeditated expedition without a raincoat or even an umbrella. The train was heading west, so only the engine driver had much of a view in that direction. It was probably distinctly louring.

Although Honeybath had left Paddington shortly after noon, he had been able to buy what was absurdly called an evening paper, and he took this unexacting reading matter along with him to the dining-car when he decided that lunch on the train was preferable to a late refection once more at the bar of the Hanwell Arms. He consumed some soup, while simultaneously absorbing what the paper had to announce about the state of the nation. It wasn't much. He turned a page, and found himself looking at Lady Munden.

Yes, here the ill-used lady was again—and again as represented by Edwin Lightfoot. This time she was presented straight, although in effective caricature; and at the bottom of the very indifferent reproduction it was just possible to read the words *Soggy Sabrina*. They rang a bell, and Honeybath was so startled by this singular bobbing up of the late Edwin Lightfoot's censurable hobby that it was moments before he realized that Lady Munden was only one in a little picture gallery of Hanwell notabilities. Next to Lady Munden was Colonel Dacre, who was labelled *Barmy Bang-bang*; next to Colonel Dacre was Michaelis, who was *Signor Cipolla*; and last came Mr Brown, who was apparently *Nasty Ned*.

Feeling (as elderly people do) that no outrage was beyond the reach of the press, Honeybath looked for justification or enlightenment in the article below the reproductions. It was a fairly reasonable recapitulation of the circumstances of Edwin Lightfoot's still recent demise, and it was more informative on the general conditions of life at Hanwell Court than concerned to speculate other than very circumspectly on exactly what had happened. That luxury accommodation for elderly gentlefolk was provided by the establishment in an impressively stylish way, and that a great deal that was mildly but expensively eccentric went on among them, were clearly the circumstances that had prompted somebody to the notion that Hanwell was good for a brisk and bright write-up. On how the drawings had come into the possession of the newspaper no information was supplied.

Through a mist of indignation, Honeybath penetrated to the fact that he *knew*. There had been reporters around remarkably soon after the discovery of Edwin's body. And there had been that break-in, and that mysterious laugh. The laugh had come when the intruder's eye had fallen, say, on Soggy Sabrina, and the scoundrel had got away with the drawings in his pocket. He must obviously have had an effective lie to tell about them when he sold his effort to an editor, since newspapers even of a rubbishing sort are chary of purchasing stolen goods. Apart from this, the thing was innocuous by the common standards of the day. Honeybath didn't at all care for it, all the same. If, as he suspected, a letter from a solicitor should presently turn up with the news that Edwin had appointed him as his executor on the professional side of his estate, that paper—he told himself—would be booked for trouble. Indeed, it could probably become a police matter at once. There had been extraordinary hardihood, surely, in such an act of pilfering within hours of Edwin's mysterious death.

Rather as if he were a demoniac figure taking the stage in grand opera, Honeybath descended from his railway carriage to the sound of great peals of distant thunder. He inquired hastily about return trains (since he wasn't going to risk another night at the Hanwell Arms) and then got himself into a cab. Just how to tackle Michaelis was something on which he hadn't made up his mind, and he realized that he had about ten minutes in which to do so now. This time, he didn't think that improvisation would quite do. Michaelis, although a less resolute man than Prout, was also a much cleverer one. If he were to be led into any betrayal of wrongdoing, a plan of campaign was required. And in the first place he had to be *seen* clearly. He had fallen into some sort of panic at the time of Edwin's death, but this didn't mean that he might not be quite a dominating personality on his own ground. Had he dominated Edwin—a pliable man in some ways, although an obstinate man in others? Honeybath felt that he knew very little about their relationship, except that Michaelis had applied what might be called the theory of occupational therapy to Edwin. In fact he had badgered him into painting—perhaps when he didn't feel in the least like it—simply to prevent his wandering round and being a nuisance. Or course, Edwin *could* be a nuisance. There had never been any doubt about that. The treatment had been extremely demeaning, all the same, and it was probable that Edwin hadn't liked it a bit. Edwin had nicknamed Michaelis Signor Cipolla. Honeybath couldn't place the reference, although he had an obscure sense that he ought to be able to do so. But it was unlikely that the original Cipolla was an amiable character.

All this didn't really get far, and it certainly didn't suggest what would be, with Michaelis, the best point of attack. It would possibly be wise to go straight to the matter of the lost pictures—and perhaps a little to stretch the probability that Charles Honeybath R.A. was going to be required to assume some legal responsibility in the administration of Edwin's estate. He'd make this point at once, and then go straight on to announce his conviction that highly suspicious circumstances were now known to him about the handling of certain important paintings which had almost certainly been in Edwin's possession until his death or very shortly before his death. Shock tactics, in fact. That would be the thing.

He found Michaelis in his Gothicized and opulently appointed room. The man didn't look well. In fact he looked like one living with something not at all comfortably to be lived with. And this, no doubt, was exactly the state of the case.

'Good afternoon,' Honeybath said. 'I think it likely that I shall be required to deal with Lightfoot's artistic affairs. The works remaining in his hands, or otherwise legally his, at the time of his death; and various questions of copyright and the like. I have reason, Dr Michaelis, to suppose—I fear I must say "suspect"—that you can help me. Do I make myself plain?'

'Far from it.' Michaelis licked his lips nervously. 'I have no idea what you're talking about.'

'I am talking, in the first place, about certain pictures painted by Lightfoot long ago, and now certainly of great value, which have disappeared. Or, rather, some have disappeared—I have reason to suppose from Hanwell Court—and their whereabouts are at present unknown to me. Others have similarly disappeared, but have turned up again where they have no business to be. In the possession, in fact, of Lightfoot's brother-in-law, Ambrose Prout. And as you now appear to enjoy Prout's more or less intimate acquaintance, I judge it likely that you know a good deal about the matter.'

'Surely at the time of Lightfoot's death his brother-in-law was his appointed, or at least customary and acknowledged, agent in the marketing and general handling of anything he produced?'

'That is, in a manner, so.' Honeybath was a shade disconcerted by this move. It had been a formidably precise statement of a very imprecise relationship. And it suggested that there might be legal snags ahead. Honeybath decided to plank more cards on the table. 'But I have to tell you, Dr Michaelis, that only this morning Prout was constrained to show me a painting of Lightfoot's, a flower-piece with zinnias, executed some twenty years ago, for which Prout could provide a provenance only of the plainest cock-and-bull sort. I think it probable that you have heard of a certain Mrs Gutermann-Seuss, who lives in Brighton. I have interviewed her, and inspected her establishment. It is clear to me that Prout has concocted supposed dealings with her which would be adequate to his all-too-evident purposes in the common commercial way, and in a situation where no grave suspicions of criminal conduct were involved. They will certainly not stand up to investigation by the police. And that investigation, I shall see to it that the police undertake. I have to remind you—and, I think, no more than remind you—that my friend has been murdered.'

'I know nothing about it!' In a sudden uncontrollable agitation, Michaelis had sprung to his feet, trembling all over. 'Prout may know. Prout is capable of anything. I don't know why your friend . . .'

'Nonsense, sir! You are deeply implicated with Prout, and you know it. *Why* was Lightfoot murdered? Plainly because he had alerted himself to the thefts in which you had both involved yourselves. You and Prout stand together. Fall together, I should rather say.'

Michaelis was silent, or silent except for a sort of snivelling. He was in the disgusting state of one totally unmanned. Honeybath gave him time. Honeybath let his gaze travel round the Medical Superintendent's well-appointed room. The Hepplewhite chairs, the Cotmans and Morlands, the Chinese pots. . . . And suddenly the strangest things were happening in Honeybath's head. Totally disparate memories were tumbling into place like a scattering of a child's building blocks miraculously ordering themselves into a coherent structure. A time-machine; a fancy he had indulged when watching Colonel Dacre crawling absurdly though a hazel thicket; this wretched Michaelis talking darkly of the resources of science. And also . . .

'Dr Michaelis,' Honeybath said, 'it is known to me—and, as it happens, to anybody who glances at a newspaper printed a few hours ago—that Lightfoot gave you a nickname. Signor Cipolla. Do you recall who Signor Cipolla is?'

'No.'

'I now do. He is a stage-hypnotist in a story by Thomas Mann. Such persons can make an adult behave as the child he once was. Or as the man he was ten, fifteen, twenty years before. While hypnotized, the subject *is* that earlier self. Please look at your mantelshelf.'

'My mantelshelf?' Michaelis stared, dully and stupidly, not at the mantelshelf but at Honeybath.

'It is in the Chinese vase standing there that Lightfoot painted his zinnias. You no doubt lent it to him when you were conducting your interesting experiments. They were astonishingly successful. You contrived—and again and again over a very considerable span of time—to throw Lightfoot into that condition in which he had once painted—and enjoyed painting, since it was painting with inspiration. Eventually you broke off the experiment as dangerous. But there the paintings were. You know nothing about such things. It would mean nothing to you that the pictures were, and yet were not, early Lightfoots. But Lightfoot himself did. It was a profoundly disturbing and undermining experience, and he took the view that you had constrained him into a unique species of forgery—something freakish and discreditable. He hid them away. But Prout found the zinnias when poking round Lightfoot's rooms. He consulted you, and discovered the bizarre truth. You then conspired together to steal all the paintings, apparently in the fond hope that Lightfoot would remain ignorant of the fact or be quite unconcerned about it.'

'There was no theft!' Michaelis had turned round and was glaring at Honeybath like a cornered rodent. 'The pictures were not properly to be regarded as belonging to Lightfoot at all. They were simply clinical material of my own, and likely to be of the greatest interest to science. I have been preparing a paper about them.'

It was as at this moment, and as if divine vengeance were about to be visited on this supreme *hubris* on the Medical Superintendent's part, that the storm broke over Hanwell Court.

XXI

THERE WERE IN fact, two storms, although some
minutes were to pass before Honeybath became confusedly
aware of the second. The first, which was veritably of the
heavens and their wrath, was confusing enough. It had
announced itself with shattering suddenness: with a crash
of thunder that seemed no farther off than the ceiling, and
which had almost instantaneously followed upon a flash of
lightning that suggested itself as having passed between
Honeybath's nose and that of his unnerved adversary. A
moment later, when Honeybath's eyesight had recovered
from the resulting black-out, he found himself alone.
Michaelis, like the bad fairy in a pantomime, had vanished
amid glare and din.

More soberly assessed, the situation simply was that he
had bolted senselessly from the room. Honeybath, vaguely
feeling that he must be intercepted before reaching Heathrow or one of the Channel ports, dashed out after him,
shouting alarms the while. These futile ejaculations were
quite drowned by the storm. The mere hiss and drumming
of the rain now descending upon the broad roofs of Hanwell
Court at the rate of several inches a minute would alone
have rendered them inoperative. But the thunder was now
hugely enjoying itself, and the lightning was laughing at the
weird concatenations of its own fiery chains.

Since the Medical Superintendent's room, although
august, was semi-subterranean, Honeybath had to run up

a staircase to reach the ground floor. He gained the hall, but lost as he did any persuasion that he was on the trail of Michaelis in an effective way. The miscreant could have disappeared in any one of a dozen directions, and under the best of conditions it would then have taken a squad of policemen to find him. But now the entire house was in considerable confusion. Inmates were scurrying about in an agitated fashion, like pampered fish in a pool into which bad children have taken to chucking stones. A general sense of mild Apocalypse or Grand Combustion had been created, and this suggestion was enhanced by a distinct smell of sulphur. This last effect, although doubtless created by natural law as a by-product of vast electrical discharge in the atmosphere, appeared to be particularly upsetting. Honeybath had a brief glimpse of the Misses Pinchon : one held a handkerchief to her noise in a despairing manner, like a damned soul ineffectively endeavouring to ward off some preliminary torment in hell; the other had sunk to her knees in prayer.

Honeybath crossed to a window commanding a view of the terraces and a long vista of park. Well-raked gravel paths were prattling brooks; the window itself streamed as if giants were hurling buckets of water at it; the skies were alive. But alive, too, was the park—with scurrying human forms. These, in two or three small clumps, were advancing upon the house at the double. For a moment Honeybath took them to be inmates, caught by the merciless elements while taking an afternoon stroll in the grounds, and now running for shelter in the luxury accommodation which was their just entitlement. But this wasn't so. They were all male. And their attire—it was possible to perceive even in their drenched conditions—was not to be associated with that of English gentlefolk. In a flash like that of the lightning itself,

Honeybath understood. Hanwell Court was under siege. Or rather not quite that. It was about to be taken by storm.

Momentarily the whole horizon blazed, then flickered. Against it in silhouette, Poseidon the Earthshaker seemed wildly to gesticulate, very much as if Hanwell Court (completed 1702) were the walls of Laomedon's Troy, about to be destroyed by the enraged divinity who hadn't been paid his bill for building them. (Troy, of course, continued to stand for some time, as Hanwell would no doubt do.)

And now something quite surprising happened. Just outside the window, Colonel Dacre appeared on the terrace, his rifle in his hand. He brought it to his shoulder, steadied himself against the balustrade, and fired. He fired, in fact, several shots with extreme rapidity. One section of the attacking force—presumably with bullets suddenly singing past their ears—scattered and took cover. Another section wheeled and disappeared within a grove of oaks, but seconds later could be briefly glimpsed again, engaged on what looked like a sinister outflanking movement designed to take the house in the rear. And now Mr Gaunt appeared beside the colonel—not armed with a *Panzerbrecher* or even a *bouche à feu*, but dragging forward an unwieldy affair which might well be his Gatling gun.

At this sight the martial spirit of Charles Honeybath (R.A.) was aroused. He flung up the window and jumped out on to the terrace. He was unarmed, but perhaps he could carry the ammunition. Now, however, there was a lull, since his more lethally equipped comrades had momentarily nothing left to fire at. Far up the drive a blaze of light—man-made, this time—appeared : the headlights, it seemed, of half a dozen cars, necessarily turned on because of the murk of the storm. Through dreadful seconds it appeared that the enemy was being overwhelmingly reinforced. Then the leading cars slowed and stopped, and helmeted policemen swarmed out of them. The effect was as of the relief of Ladysmith or Mafeking.

Yet within Hanwell Court itself it was suddenly clear that all was not well. It had been taken, or at least successfully breached from the rear! There were shouts, there was uproar, from the staircase; shots rang out and bullets sang; through the open window now behind Honeybath there appeared the figure of Mr Brown, fleeing in terror from some outrageous pursuit. He vaulted the balustrade and vanished, with hard on his heels two or three of the attacking force. One of these, Honeybath fleetingly recognized as an acquaintance. It was the person with whom he had been so disagreeably constrained to converse in the bar of the Hanwell Arms.

But now the police were everywhere. They were swamping Hanwell—just as the gang, apparently joined by other gangs, had been proposing to swamp it. There were no more shots. The assailants (disappointingly tamely, Honeybath caught himself feeling) were giving in.

But where was Brown—so plainly the sole quarry of the operation? The answer came fairly soon, and just as the storm, with a surprising suddenness, passed away. Beneath clearing skies, Adamson (who was in charge of the police) took Honeybath to have a look at Brown. This required a walk through puddles to the end of the avenue. There, Poseidon and his sea-monster had disappeared from their pedestal. Zeus, as if fed up with his brother's histrionics, had unloosed a thunderbolt. The Earthshaker had fallen as a pile of shattered marble. And he had fallen upon, and crushed to extinction, the one-time owner of an immaculate Panama hat.

XXII

'HE KILLED YOUR friend,' Adamson said soberly.
Rather surprisingly, he had carried Honeybath off to the
Hanwell Arms. Rather more surprisingly, they were both
consuming alcoholic liquor out of licensed hours, although
in the decent seclusion of a private room.

'Killed Edwin—why?' Not unnaturally, Honeybath was
completely bewildered.

'He'd seen that caricature—the one those villains saw in
the paper today.'

'Nasty Ned?'

'Narky Ned.' Adamson had frowned at the inaccuracy.

'Of course. It looked like 'Nasty' in the reproduction. But
I remember. Narky Ned. It was rather excessive, wasn't it—
killing Edwin because of that?' Honeybath knew he was
being absurd. 'Brown must have been an uncommonly
sensitive man.'

'Nothing of the kind. Brown was extremely stupid, among
other things. He'd heard Lightfoot say something about an
exhibition of his entire works.'

'That was nonsense. Just one of Edwin's odd jokes.'

'Then it was an expensive one. Brown was stupid, as I
say. He'd also gathered that Lightfoot was by way of
sending some of those drawings for temporary view to
exhibitions here and there.'

'That was true. Lady Munden. And also . . .'

'Yes, yes, Mr Honeybath. The point is that Brown

couldn't afford to let it be known that he lived here. *We* couldn't let it be known, for that matter. We'd thought up Hanwell Court as the unlikeliest place in the world for him. Just right for holding him safe and sound for years.'

'*Narky* Ned?' One of Honeybath's flashes, his inspirations, had come to him. 'But how did Edwin know Brown was a nark?'

'Intuition, no doubt. Something you artists manage. Of course Brown ought to have contacted us, and we'd have whisked him away somewhere else. Stupidity again. But I was stupid myself. I ought to have removed him as soon as trouble of any sort blew up at Hanwell Court. But he was an awkward man to deal with, was Brown. He said he liked it here.'

'So he did.'

'After killing Lightfoot, he must have planned to do a rummage and collect that caricature as soon as things quietened down. Only, some unprincipled reporter got in before him.'

'You regarded Brown as an important man?'

'My dear sir, he was England's Number One Informer. Nothing he didn't know. If you lost your watch to a pick-pocket, he'd tell you the chap's name at once. Marvellous sense, too, of *modus operandi*. Take a glance at a busted strong-room, and pin-point the whole operation. A great loss to us.'

'Lightfoot's death is a great loss to me.'

'Of course, Mr Honeybath. And I'm very sorry. So fortuitous, too. Of course Prout and Michaelis never had a thought of killing your friend. They were just going to do their quiet grab, and think to get away with it. If Lightfoot did give trouble, Michaelis could probably find a colleague who could be convinced your friend was totally mad and raving. Lightfoot's actual death must have been a terrific shock to them. It put them right out on a limb.'

'They *are* on a limb? They can be prosecuted?'

'I suppose so.' Adamson sounded doubtful and not very interested.

'Michaelis had the astounding impudence to tell me the pictures must really be regarded as belonging to him anyway. As part of his clinical material.'

'A clever barrister could make a good deal of that, don't you think? However, we'll consider trying to put them both inside. We'll consider it most carefully.'

'Mr Adamson, you do understand the entire outrageous affair as I've given it to you? That my friend was treated like a guinea-pig? That he was put in great distress of mind by it? And that those scoundrels then had the wonderful thought that they'd make money out of it?'

'I understand all that.'

'And that, if they'd succeeded, falsely dated works by my friend would have gone on the market? That eventually it might appear as if he had skilfully produced a species of counterfeit of his own earlier work?'

'Well, Mr Honeybath, at least nothing of the sort can happen now. The man Prout can certainly be forced to resign those pictures—even if only as part of a bargain.'

'An undertaking not to prosecute him, you mean? Wouldn't that be compounding a felony—or whatever the legal phrase may be?'

'I think not. Tax evasion and unobtrusive tax recovery strike me as an analogy. But we'd have to be sure of our ground, of course. Consult high legal authority, as we regularly do. We don't break the law, you know. It would be a self-stultifying thing to do.'

'What about Brown? Were there charges you knew you could have brought against him?'

'No—or not with any assurance of success. He'd done his time for one thing and another. And he must have had a wretched time of it, don't you think? He knew who were out to get him.'

'But they didn't succeed.'

'That's true. But the just gods did, Mr Honeybath. He was killed by what I understand to have been quite a considerable work of art. There's a kind of poetic justice in that.'

'I suppose so.' Honeybath glanced at his watch. He was feeling extremely tired. Adamson noticed the action.

'Are you intending to go back to London tonight, Mr Honeybath?'

'Most certainly I am. And never to see Hanwell Court again.'

'That's very understandable.' Adamson, an acute man if not a wholly sympathetic one, may have felt that this eminent painter had had enough of coppers and narks alike. 'I wonder,' he asked, 'whether I might provide a car to take you home? It might be simpler than the train.'

Honeybath drained his glass and got to his feet.

'Thank you,' he said. 'I'd be most grateful.'